THE BARRISTER'S CHALLENGE

CHALLENGE

HEIRS OF BERKSHIRE BOOK TWO

KAREN LYNNE

A Barrister's Challenge

Heirs of Berkshire Book Two

OTHER BOOKS BY KAREN LYNNE

Brides of Somerset Series

Heirs of Berkshire Series

Join my reader's group and enjoy updates for new books and little bits of tidbits on 19th-century history.

CHAPTER 1

WALTER LONGMAN SPLASHED, spattering mud and grime into the air, as his carriage cut through central London.

The rain had been relentless these past few weeks. As miserable as it was, he supposed it reflected his mood as of late. He peered out the carriage window at the London streets, trying to ignore the pain in his heart when he dwelt on what he'd lost. He'd thought he'd put Patience Hawthorn out of his heart when their engagement failed because of her parents' refusal. He realized now he'd always held onto a small hope that things would turn around once he established himself as a respectable barrister.

Instead, he'd had to watch from afar, reading snippets of her goings-on and rumors of a betrothal to another. Still, she haunted his thoughts constantly.

The carriage came to a stop near Lincoln's Inn, the

inn of court in which he belonged, forcing him to pull his musing away from the lady. Today was an important one for his career. He was on the list to be one of the chosen barristers to take part in a large case within the Circuit Courts. Should he win, he'd establish credibility and a larger wage.

Walter stepped out onto the street, narrowly missing a large puddle, before he paid the driver. The carriage rolled away, horse's hooves clacking as Walter's eyes swept the street. Parasols protected the delicate heads of the women, and the men ducked forward, letting the rain droplets fall on the brim of their hats. Walter had donned his own black cloak and top hat, keeping it low over his eyes.

As he took his first steps toward his offices, a blue bonnet caught his attention. He turned, watching as a woman passed near him, clutching a reticule. Her auburn curls escaped under the bonnet's confines.

Walter's heart leaped into his throat. It couldn't be— was it? He had to know.

Ducking his head down, he followed the woman, trying to glimpse her face. The blue gown and bonnet reminded him of soft hands, whispered promises, and full pink lips.

She stopped at the corner of the street, fidgeting in her reticule. The curve of her shoulders, her pale neck—

Walter was only yards away from her now, so close to reaching out and delicately touching her elbow.

As she turned, Walter stopped in his tracks. The face was unfamiliar, spotted with dark freckles, the chin too pointed, lips thin. She was not Patience.

His heart deflated, and he scowled at the wet, filthy ground. Thunder rumbled and the sprinkle of rain quickly became a deluge. People hurried around him, trying to get to their destinations without becoming soaked through. The woman quickly crossed the street, meeting up with a man who wrapped an arm around her, pulling her under a protecting umbrella.

Walter remained frozen, his jaw clenched, willing her memory away. He felt people brush against his shoulders, trying to get past him.

"Mr. Longman!" The voice was loud in Walter's ears.

He turned, lowering his eyes to a man who stood a foot shorter than he.

The man raised his thick gray brows.

"Aiming to catch a cold?" When Walter didn't respond, he reached up to pat Walter on the back. "Let me walk with you."

He didn't argue. Mr. Welch had been a mentor to Walter, taking him on when no one else would. He had quickly become like a second father. Together, they walked toward Lincoln's Inn, the rain hissing past their ears.

Stepping inside, Walter removed his wet hat and shook it off.

Mr. Welch chuckled, clutching the top of his cane.

"If I didn't know any better, I'd say you were quite turned around back there, Mr. Longman."

"Thought I spotted an old acquaintance."

Walter removed his cloak, trying to sound nonchalant, but winced at his own words. *Friend... affianced... acquaintance.* Funny how relationships changed. He shook his head, trying to clear his thoughts again.

Mr. Welch snorted. "Get to work, you heart-sick loon."

Walter frowned, but the well-respected barrister only chuckled.

"You think I don't notice how you mope around? Clearly, you've been jilted. Take my advice—stay a bachelor as long as you can." Mr. Welch tapped his cane against Walter's ankles and winked before moving down the hall to his office.

Walter clenched his jaw as he retreated to his own office, guarded by a heavy oak door with his name on a gold-trimmed plaque. He hung his coat and hat, then sat behind his desk, trying to sort his thoughts. It wasn't working. Patience had captured almost every moment of his thoughts since finding out she'd gone to the east end of London only a week ago. He scowled as he remembered Lord Berkshire, Patience's intended, sitting directly across from him in this very room, accusing him of intentionally putting Patience in harm's way.

Frustration flared in Walter's breast. The very thought! Lord Berkshire didn't know how lucky he was to be courting her. It still hurt that Patience was with another man, and he was beside himself at knowing how to wrench his thoughts away from the woman.

He extracted a file documenting the case he hoped to be assigned, riffling through the papers. He'd almost memorized every detail, trying to purge his thoughts of Patience.

Hugh Vanderbilt had been implicated in murder. Should Walter get the case, he would prove Mr. Vanderbilt's guilt. The man they accused him of murdering had been the heir to the Viscount of Highfield. Walter had met the future Viscount once, and in his mind, the world was better off without the man. It would be tricky, but if Walter succeeded, it would assure his career. He'd become more sought after by ladies who wanted a comfortable living.

He didn't blame Patience for her parents' refusal of his proposal. But it still irked him that she leaped into this year's season, and only weeks later found herself the most eligible bachelor in London.

She claimed she didn't care for money when Walter courted her. It looked like things had changed. Her being with an earl only added insult to injury, clarifying that she had set her sights much higher than he could attain.

Hang it, Walter thought, swiping a hand through his hair. *Enough.* He would not let thoughts of Patience impede his career. He banished her from his mind once and for all, spending the next hour pouring over the case notes.

Walter pulled his watch out of his pocket and glanced at it, letting it dangle without putting it back. He leaped from his chair, gathering the file and his fountain pens before rushing out of his office.

He was about to be late.

He worked his way down the hall until he found the meeting room where a handful of barristers vying for the case gathered around a table, shuffling through the same notes that Walter had just been immersed in.

Mr. Welch patted an empty seat next to him, and Walter sat, eyeing his competition. Three of them would be chosen, and he was the most inexperienced of them all. He swallowed, trying to keep his confidence high. Mr. Bamber sat across from him at the long, polished table, looking relaxed, grinning at his competitors the way a fox grins at plump chickens. He caught Walter's gaze, and his grin spread wider.

Walter held the man's gaze, refusing to blink. Mr. Bamber's eyebrows arched, accepting the challenge.

The lead barrister, Mr. Conrad, entered the room, black robes ruffling behind him, his wig askew.

"Gentlemen," he paused, taking a seat at the head of the table. "We have many interested parties and not much time." He slammed a stack of papers onto the table. "Mr. Vanderbilt's case. Who would like to be on the team?"

Walter stood, along with four other men his senior, including Mr. Bamber.

Mr. Conrad's weathered gray eyes swept over the room. "Briefly describe why you would excel at the case. Mr. Bamber, you begin first."

Mr. Bamber's dark eyes glittered. "I have been a member of this council for fifteen years. I've undertaken the most difficult of cases and always succeed. I am the most qualified among us to take on the case."

Walter couldn't believe the man's overconfidence. He looked to Mr. Conrad to see if he was at all impressed. His gaze was fixed steadily on Mr. Bamber.

"Bamber, I recall several cases you've lost. Yet you claim to have won them all."

Mr. Bamber's smile grew forced. His pride had been wounded.

Mr. Conrad turned to a middle-aged man Walter knew as Mr. Mosby, a well-respected barrister. He looked from Walter to Mr. Bamber, then chuckled, sitting.

"I think I will sit this one out, actually." Mr. Mosby smiled.

All eyes turned to Walter and Mr. Welch. Walter swallowed, forcing himself to remain calm. Patience must have rattled him more than he thought. Mr. Welch gave him an encouraging nod.

"I am the youngest among you." Walter looked to Mr. Conrad but kept his head held high. "But I have gained respect quickly on this council. I've taken on smaller cases, but each one *had* been a success. I get to the core of a case, and fight for the truth. It's time to focus my talents on something bigger, if you'll allow me." He dipped his head humbly in Mr. Conrad's direction.

Mr. Welch spoke up, holding a finger in the air. "I second the motion. Mr. Longman has been most attentive this past year. I have confidence in his abilities to handle this case."

Mr. Conrad nodded, his finger tapping his gray beard before he stopped and adjusted his wig, skewing it the other direction. "Very well, then. I will assign you, Mr. Welch, to work alongside Mr. Longman on this case." His gaze turned to a sour Mr. Bamber. "If Mr. Longman cannot handle it, I will reassign you to be the lead, Bamber. Are we all clear?"

The men in the room uttered a sound of agreement and then adjourned.

As Walter strode triumphantly out of the office, Mr. Bamber caught up to him.

"Well done, my friend, though I hope you understand what kind of case you've gotten yourself into. It's not for the faint of heart."

Walter forced a smile. "I suppose time will tell." He hastened away from Mr. Bamber, heading back to his office to review the case note again.

He picked up the paper he had purchased that morning, flipping it open to peruse the political atmosphere, but his eyes caught the name of Lord Berkshire. He stilled, reading it carefully. Patience's name stood out like a beacon that his heart seemed irrevocably drawn to.

Lord Berkshire and Patience's courtship had not ended in marriage? Patience taken from London early, hastily, her name muddied? His heart pounded in his chest as he continued to read. Scandal had followed her back to the country.

Walter knew instantly that her misguided adventure in traveling to the slums of the east end of London had something to do with it. Lord Berkshire had burst into his office, accusing him, of all people, of sending her there. The man had seemed to care about her safety. Did it end there? Was Lord Berkshire so upset at Patience's careless behavior that it would take his affections away from her? If it had, the man was a fool.

His head throbbed. He'd been distracted today. His attentions divided. The woman didn't deserve to take up so much space in his heart. He winced, shoving the thought from his mind. He couldn't bother himself with Patience any longer. He needed all his mental faculties to prove a man's guilt, and he was more determined now than ever to do so. But the things he'd read made little sense. Something was terribly wrong.

CHAPTER 2

PATIENCE LOOKED TO HER MOTHER, imploring her to see reason. She didn't know why she tried. Her mother had always been unyielding with anything having to do with Walter Longman.

"Why can't I attend Juliana's wedding?"

"Because she is the cause of the trouble we're experiencing, and the reason we have returned to the country. I absolutely forbid you to attend their wedding." Her mother sniffed.

Patience received an invitation from her dear friend Juliana, inviting her to her upcoming wedding, and she desperately wanted to attend. She'd been in the country for a month now.

"If we had not fled, we could have weathered their engagement. I have refused to marry the earl. It was perfectly acceptable, and a lady's prerogative, to refuse a gentleman's proposal."

"Not to an earl. I don't understand you," her mother complained. "You would have been a countess. Instead, you prefer a tradesman."

"Walter is not a tradesman. It is perfectly honorable to study the law." Patience knew it still upset her mother that Juliana and her newly intended tricked her parents into believing the earl was pursuing Patience.

It had been a ruse they had all agreed upon to get society to give Lord Berkshire some breathing room while he was grieving his father's loss, and a way for Patience's mother to stop nagging her about accepting a suitable offer of marriage, one her mother would approve.

It had brought Juliana and Lord Berkshire together. They were blissfully happy and preparing for a wedding. Her parents returned to the country in disgrace after her mother had eavesdropped at the door, thus uncovering their scheme.

Patience didn't mind, except that Walter was still in London, believing she had abandoned their love. Although she had tried, they had resolved nothing.

Patience bit her tongue. It wouldn't help to provoke her mother.

"Juliana is the kindest of friends. She was trying to

help. We hoped you would understand my feelings for Walter."

"Ha!" her mother's attention returned to her needlepoint.

Patience turned to her father. His eyes fixed within the pages of his book. "Papa, won't you let me attend?"

Her father sank deeper into his chair, his book obscuring his face.

"Listen to your mama, Patience."

Why did she try? Her father always sided with her mother. He was cowed by his wife, afraid to stand up to her demands.

Patience's mouth clamped shut. She folded Juliana's invitation and stood. Walking through the door, briskly moving up the stairs to her room.

Closing the door behind her, she grabbed a pillow and tossed it across the room with a low rumble. It hit the wall and fell to the floor with an unsatisfactory thud.

Patience collapsed on her bed, staring up at the pale silk canopy. She hated it here, hated her mother's control over her. She loathed writing Juliana to inform her she would not be attending her wedding and wondered if she could find a way to leave, even without her parents'

permission. There was no use reasoning with her mother, who wouldn't be persuaded to let her marry the man she loved. Couldn't she see that attending the wedding would silence the gossip?

Could she not remember her youth? But her mother had never been young, she was sure of it.

Walter invaded her thoughts as he invariably did. It hurt to know he was in London, working hard at a respectable profession, while she was back here in Wallingford.

Patience wondered if Walter had received the letter she'd written explaining the truth about her and Lord Berkshire. He hadn't responded.

Or had he?

Her mother could have taken a letter without her knowledge. Her heart sank at the possibility. It was something she would do.

Did he still think of her? Long for her the way she did for him? She hugged a pillow, feeling her throat constrict as hot tears stung her eyes. Unable to sit still a moment longer, she moved to her secretary. Drawing a fresh piece of paper, she picked up her pen. Surely, he wouldn't think ill of her for writing. He had asked for her hand. Had it not been for her parents' refusal, she would be married to the gentleman she loved.

Hesitation hung as she bit at her bottom lip. She carefully penned, *"My dear Walter…"*

She scribbled another two sentences, then crossed them out, frustrated. What more could she say that hadn't been said in her last letter to him just before leaving London? She'd explained her side of the story—that she did not love Lord Berkshire and never had. The Earl loved her friend Juliana. Perhaps she could write Walter and tell him of the impending wedding.

Her hand hovered over the blank parchment, a dollop of ink hanging from the tip of her pen.

If he hadn't responded to her first letter, would he care at all about Lord Berkshire and Juliana? Would he care about her?

She blotted the ink before she wrote, *"I am trapped in a cage of suppressed emotion and unrequited love."*

It was a bit dramatic and not like her at all.

She stared bitterly at her words before crumpling the paper and giving up and tossing the wad across the room. It was useless writing Walter another letter she doubted he would respond to.

A knock sounded on her door.

"Patience, come to dinner at once."

Her brow creased as her mother moved away, footfalls echoing down the hall. She knew why a servant hadn't been sent to fetch her. Her mother wanted to wield her control. Let Patience know she would not be ignored. As melodramatic as it seemed, Patience wanted to stay locked up in her room, pining after a man she could not have while silently rebelling against her mother's iron fist.

She didn't care if she starved.

But she was a coward like her father, not daring to cross her mother. She made her way reluctantly down the stairs and into the dining room. Her parents were already seated, not bothering to wait as a servant set food in front of them. Patience took her seat at the left of her father, across from her mother, refusing to look at them. She sat in silence, not bothering to make conversation. It didn't matter, her father was reading the paper, her mother buttering her bread.

"Oh," her father's startled outburst, stopped both women from finishing their bites.

All eyes turned to him. It was a rare occurrence to have her father make any sounds over dinner.

"Well. What is it?" her mother asked testily when it became apparent that her father was not going to enlighten them on his own.

Her father squinted, continuing his reading, not bothering to acknowledge her mother's annoyed tone. He cleared his throat, not looking at either of them.

"Daniel Longman has passed away," he breathed, a troubled expression on his brow.

Patience's stomach lurched, upsetting the food that had settled there.

"Walter's brother?" she whispered.

"How did he die?" Her mother seemed interested.

Patience was, though most likely for different

reasons. Her mother always had to be in the know so she could be the first to spread the best bits of gossip to the women of the neighborhood.

"Carriage accident, it seems." His concerned eyes raised from the paper.

Patience exchanged a glance with her mother. Was that distress she saw?

"A carriage accident? How?" Her mother's voice broke.

"It's vague." Her father shrugged. Folding the newspaper, he set it beside his plate.

Patience snatched it up before her mother could say any more on the subject. She flipped through the pages, finding the story and reading over as she discovered the details for herself.

"Poor Walter," she murmured.

Her father tore a chunk of bread with his fingers.

"He's set to inherit his family's estate now that his brother has passed," he mumbled to himself.

Patience's eyes widened. She swallowed as her mind raced. Walter would be heartbroken.

Her mother's eyes drilled into her father's. "Unlikely he'll claim it. He's too busy becoming a barrister in London."

"He must return home to sort out the family affairs. He has his younger sister to look after." His eyes grew distant. "As well as his mother. He wouldn't abandon them." He shook his head, as if coming out of a fog.

Her father's words replayed in her head. *He'll need to return home.* Walter would return to Wallingford, if only for a little while to set his affairs in order. He now had an estate on his hands. Not as wealthy as Lord Berkshire's ,but enough to settle down — Patience's eyes returned to her mother.

Her eyes narrowed, watching Patience. She hissed, throwing her napkin onto the table. "*No,* Patience, you are not to carry on with that man under any circumstances."

"I would never *carry on*, Mama!" Heat rose to her cheeks at the implication. How could her own mother have such a low opinion of her? And why was her mother so against Walter?

"I only thought he might be more appealing to you now that he has inherited his family's estate." Her voice dripped with sarcasm, but her mother didn't seem to notice.

Her father cleared his throat. "There are advantages to Patience and Mr. Longman's union," he said, coming to her defense for the first time in her life.

Both Patience and her mother gaped openly.

He lowered his eyes. "There are advantages to having such a connection. For example, we could combine our estates. I would have thought you'd welcome the rise in status." He looked at his wife. "And it'd keep Patience close."

He looked away as if he knew what the response would be. But Patience just gawked, as she hadn't seen him so sensible in years.

Her mother's eyes were piercing; Patience feared her father would be sliced into ribbons. "We've already turned him away. Patience will have more suitable suitors."

"But I don't *want* any other suitors—" Patience argued, but her mother's piercing glare silenced her.

"We will end this discussion here and now," her mother spit out after a strained silence. She turned her attention to her roast duck, acting as if nothing had happened. "I'm thinking of adding cabbage to the garden this year." She turned to her father. "Is that not a good idea?"

Patience looked to her father, but he'd already settled into submission. "Whatever you like, dear."

She would have thought it comical had they not been discussing her future. Patience dropped her napkin onto the table and stood. Her appetite had fled. She swept from the room, not bothering to ask permission to leave.

Her thoughts were on Daniel's sudden death. The heartache Walter must be feeling. Life was so fragile. It could be taken instantly. She felt his loss keenly as she trudged up the steps, seeking the solitude of her room.

She rested on her bed, her heart beating against her chest. Walter returning to Wallingford unsettled her, yet a small bit of hope rose to her chest. She could talk to him face to face. Resolve things, find out why he wouldn't return her letters. If he chose not to forgive her, he would know she still cared. She'd never stopped loving him. Her chest constricted, thinking of the pain she must have caused when feigning a courtship with Lord Berkshire.

A terrible thought pierced her. What if he'd found another? Someone he cared for in London?

She banished the image from her mind, unwilling to think of the possibility. No need to dwell on something before knowing the facts. Instead, she focused on seeing Walter again. No matter that her mother had forbidden it. She would find a way to comfort Walter during his time of grief. Thoughts of seeing him lifted her spirits. She would make things right. This whole incident would be but a painful memory. Walter was not so unfeeling as to deny her an audience and allow her to explain.

CHAPTER 3

WALTER LOCKED his office door before moving to Mr. Welch's rooms. He stood outside the office staring at the closed door, his throat dry. He had no idea if he would still have a seat on the case once he announced the news. He couldn't change the situation; he needed to return home. As the new heir, he had certain responsibilities. His mind still spun with the news he had received by post that morning. It was most unexpected, tragic, and very poor timing.

He knocked on the door, his muscles rigid. He had worked too hard to get where he was, he would not let his position go without a fight. The door opened. Mr. Welch stood in his robes, his hair askew. The startled expression in his eyes made Walter smile for a moment before he remembered his purpose.

The man blinked at Walter, yawning as he moved back, a telling sign he'd just woken from a nap.

"Come in, Mr. Longman."

Walter obeyed, but stood while Mr. Welch tidied his appearance. Walter fingered his top hat, shifting from side to side. Mr. Welch took a moment, then turned, his brows creased into a frown.

"Is something the matter?"

"I'm afraid so." Walter swallowed, wetting his dry throat. "My brother... I just found out this morning... has passed away."

Mr. Welch's features shifted, his eyes dark and somber. "I am sorry to hear that."

Walter's jaw tightened, dreading what he had to say next. "I must go to Wallingford. Settle his affairs, you understand."

If this man posed any resistance, he was prepared to argue. Lay the facts at his feet and plead his case as to why he was still the best man for the job.

Mr. Welch nodded. "I understand. Of course you must. It will interfere with the Vanderbilt case," he fingered his chin.

"I still plan to work," Walter said quickly. "But I'll need a little more time. If you could send me regular letters concerning the case, I would be much obliged."

Walter held his breath, hoping the man would offer no resistance.

"It is highly irregular." Mr. Welch scratched at his beard. "I will see what I can do. But hurry back, Mr. Longman, or the council will be forced to assign someone else in your stead."

Walter stepped forward, locking his gaze with Mr. Welch's.

"I need this case," he said quietly. "You understand that?"

"I do." Mr. Welch clapped Walter on the shoulder. "Do what you must in Wallingford. I will hold down the fort, as they say, until your return."

"Thank you." A rush of relief flooded him.

It had not been as hard as he'd expected to assure his holdings. It shouldn't have surprised him. Mr. Welch had been a steady mentor and friend. Encouraging Walter as he traversed the waters of his chosen career.

Mr. Welch offered his hand, and Walter clasped it tightly, giving it a firm shake.

"Safe travels." Mr. Welch smiled. "I'll send specifics of any additional details by special courier."

Walter nodded, a new relief within his chest. The constriction he'd felt upon hearing the news loosened.

"Thank you, I shall return as soon as I am able. I will not rest until I find what truly happened to the deceased in the case. I fear there is something even more nefarious than we supposed. I'll find the proof."

Mr. Welsh's smile broadened. "I knew you would. I have every confidence you will sniff out any misdeeds."

Walter returned to his small loft on the third floor above a dress shop. A small space adequate for him, which is how he liked it—until he found a wife. One who would appreciate his career.

Patience's lovely face swam in his memory. She did not have the strength of character he needed in a wife. Hadn't she proven it with her actions? Womanhood had weakened her, though he treasured his memories of the spirited girl from his youth.

He pulled a trunk from beneath his bed and threw his clothing inside, not heeding the items he packed as his memory wandered to his brother.

Daniel was gone.

It didn't seem possible. His healthy elder brother gone so young, in the prime of his life. A vibrant man of thirty and single. No family to mourn except his sister Henrietta—what must she be feeling? His heart ached at the thought of her grief, and his mother would be shattered at the loss.

His family was close. Especially after illness took their father, and now his brother. Walter grit his teeth and quickly finished packing. He would leave first thing tomorrow on the morning stage. It was not a full-day's journey to Wallingford, his childhood home. He could be there by afternoon.

Patience, she would be there. He slammed his trunk closed. He mustn't think of her, not on top of everything else that was going on in his life. She would be one more worry that needn't concern him.

———

Henrietta flung the door wide in her rush to greet Walter as he pulled up to the family estate. It wasn't large, but still held credible status among the neighbors. Well-manicured greenery surrounded the home, and a small fishing pond lay nestled behind the house. He was in charge of only a handful of tenants, and they hired villager men to maintain the grounds. A property to be proud of.

Henrietta's golden blonde tendrils were tied back from her face, a few escaping the large red bow tied at the back of her head. She rushed toward him once he set his feet on firm ground, hiding her face in the crook of his neck. Walter held his fifteen-year-old sister. The reality of their loss settled in.

His mother stood at the front door, her face splotchy and eyes distant, evidence she'd been crying.

Walter pulled back, brushing away a tear that slid down Henrietta's face.

"It will be alright," he whispered.

She nodded, swatting her eyes. Walter wrapped an

arm around her shoulders, leading her through the front
door. Reaching around his mother with his other arm, he
pulled her into a hug. She trembled in his embrace.

Daniel was dead.

His heart tightened.

Walter was head of the family now and must buoy
the family in their grief.

After a few minutes of silence punctuated by a few
sniffles, his mother pulled away and gestured them into
the drawing room.

"Come, Walter. You must be exhausted from your
journey."

He followed behind her into the parlor, noting
antiques he didn't remember propped resolutely against
the walls. Original paintings hung throughout the room,
papered in neutral colors.

Though there were more things, the room seemed
darker than he remembered. He sat in front of his
mother, molding into the leather winged-back chair.

"How was your journey?" his mother asked.

"As expected, long and dull." He tried for a smile
but found he couldn't when looking into his mother's
grief-stricken face. "How did it happen?" he asked
quietly.

Henrietta let out a shuddering whimper. But his
mother proceeded to give him the details.

"Daniel took the carriage out, as he so often does,

but this time—" her grief-stricken eyes found his. "We're not sure, but the carriage rolled down the side of a ravine. A wheel had fallen off. The carriage must have been faulty, as it was relatively new." Her face caved. "He was crushed."

The image played in Walter's mind: his brother, happily guiding the horses down the road, then being jerked off the cliff as the carriage broke down. Walter ground his teeth, hoping his elder brother hadn't suffered much pain in the end.

"The neighbors found him," Henrietta whispered, her head on their mother's shoulder.

Walter cleared his throat. "Have you made any arrangements for the funeral?"

Her head shook. "We wanted to wait for you."

He nodded. "I will take care of everything. You have no more need to worry. I am sorry I was not here when it happened, so I could have comforted you sooner."

"Thank you. I shall rest easier knowing you are here."

He gave his mother a half smile, his nerves on their last thread. He would look at the accounts, then go to his room and wash the dust from his journey.

"Where did Daniel keep the accounts? I need to check the state of affairs before I can move forward," he asked.

His mother nodded. "Daniel keeps the books in the library."

Walter stood. "I will be in the library then."

His mother frowned. "Won't you rest first?"

He shook his head. "I'm needed in London. They have assigned me an important case. If it ends satisfactorily, I can give you and Henrietta the comfort that is your due. The sooner I can handle Daniel's affairs, the better." He approached his mother, giving her a quick kiss. "I'll be down for dinner."

She reached for his arm, stopping his progress. "Daniel kept us in every comfort. I am sure you can finish your business in London and have a very comfortable life here in Wallingford."

He stiffened, looking about finding new trinkets in the room. Something was amiss. He knew the estate income was stretched and could not handle lavish spending. It was the reason he'd trained in the law.

He mounted the stairs and entered the library to a keen sense of nostalgia. This had been his father's study before he'd died. Closing his eyes, Walter inhaled the scent of oak and worn leather books.

The large desk he'd hide under as a boy stood empty. Walter shut the door and approached, running his hand over its smooth, hard surface. He took a moment to compose himself, then sat behind the sturdy bureau, pulling out the drawers one by one.

He found the account books tucked inside the drawer to his right. Taking a deep breath, he opened the ledger and read, finding receipts wedged between the pages. His mother had been right—Daniel purchased the carriage for a handsome sum last year. He frowned at the manufacturer's name. Because of their faulty product, his brother was dead. A strong desire to take them to court mounted as he handled the receipt.

Before he could let blame be placed, his lawyer brain took over, needing proof before he disparaged anyone's name. He'd take a look at the wrecked carriage himself to determine what had happened. It could have been negligence on Daniel's part, as hard as that was to consider.

He continued to peruse through the receipts, then moved to the ledger, checking the figures recorded. His heart plummeted. His stomach churned. He stared at the final and most recent sum. The spending exceeded the estate's income and had been for years. The estate was a mess, mortgaged against the debt. Walter's jaw clenched, flipping back through the receipts. How could Daniel have been so reckless? Why hadn't he been told? And why did Daniel continue making unnecessary purchases, knowing he couldn't pay?

A soft knock sounded, and Walter closed the book.

His mother's head peeked through the open door.

"Did you find what you were looking for?" she asked, motherly concern taking precedence over her grief.

"Yes." Walter hoped his voice didn't betray his concern.

"The vicar has just arrived. Would you like to talk to him?"

Walter nodded as he stood. His head spun with the recent information he had gained. "I'll be down in a moment."

She gave him a sad smile. "It is so good to have you home. I have missed your steady influence."

"I have missed you too." He stood. Walking toward his mother, he gave her another embrace, thankful she was still in his life.

As she closed the door behind her, he braced himself against the desk, hissing out a breath. *"Daniel, what were you doing?"*

They would have to go into further debt to pay for the funeral, and he was now responsible for paying the debts.

It weighed heavily on his shoulders. The case in London became even more important now. No, it was critical to secure his future. Taking a deep breath, he straightened and prepared to talk with the vicar.

CHAPTER 4

IT HAD BEEN three days since he'd returned home, and the funeral arrangements were in place. With time on his hands, Walter was itching to leave the house. The thoughts of Patience, only two miles down the road, gave him pause. Did she grieve the loss of her relationship with Lord Berkshire more than theirs?

He shook his head, vanquishing Patience from his mind. He'd kept thoughts of her at bay since having arrived with all that he had to do. He hadn't the desire to make a habit of thinking of her now that time was his.

Henrietta had been playing the pianoforte non-stop for the past few days. He reasoned it was her way of grieving, but the solemn music dampened his mood. He had seen little of his mother. He imagined she remained in her room or the library to hide away from the reality of having her eldest ripped from her. He left the house to clear his head as he wandered the grounds, deep in thought.

He made his way to the fishing pond just below the estate, walking among the cattails, watching the sunlight glisten on the surface. He could see the little shack at the edge of their property where the groundskeeper kept the fishing and boating equipment.

He pulled Patience inside the shack when he was only twelve, she ten. They'd used it as headquarters for their imagined investigator bureau. They'd find some insignificant mystery to solve and meet up in the small shed, discussing clues and theories. He remembered the way her hair frizzed, a tangled mess she could never control. Her nose sprinkled with freckles, though they'd dimmed as the years passed. Now the red highlights of her auburn hair shown and she'd grown into a beauty.

A movement drew Walter from the memory as a groom, in the distance, disappeared into the stables.

He remembered the faulty carriage. If anyone knew where it was now, it would be the stable hands. Walter moved to the stables, shoving his hands in his pockets.

The old groom was busy cleaning a stall. He remembered Benjamin, a loyal servant who had been with them since before his father's passing.

He turned to see Walter. Resting his arms on his shovel, he wiped his brow. "Master Walter, I heard you had returned. 'Tis a sad day to be sure."

"It is Benjamin." Horses stood in their stalls, but no carriage was in view. How had the horses fared?

He pushed past the thickness in his chest. "I came to ask about the carriage my brother drove at the time of his death. Did you happen to see it... after?" He cleared his throat, pulling in his emotions.

Benjamin nodded, his face drooping. "The younger hands loaded the wreckage and delivered it to the blacksmith the day you arrived. Not much could be done to repair it."

"What did the blacksmith want with it?"

"Well, 'twas no use to us, sir." Benjamin grabbed a pitchfork and began stabbing hay bales, sending fresh hay to the horses. "I reckon he'd want to use some parts for his work. Your mother sold it for scrap."

Anxiety clutched at Walter. Was he too late? Had the blacksmith destroyed all the clues of his brother's death?

"How did the carriage look?" he asked. "I was told it was missing a wheel."

"Yes, sir. Missing the right wheel, and the top had caved completely in. The underside was all bent up, it was."

"What do you suppose caused the wheel to come off?"

Benjamin shrugged, tossing the last bit of hay. "Heaven only knows. Could've hit some boulder or a hole in the road. Or maybe the wheel was coming off already. I suppose we'll never know for sure."

Walter clenched his jaw. "Thank you, Benjamin."

He strode from the stable, his mind on finding the truth. He needed to go to the blacksmith's and investigate the carriage, but it was getting late and tomorrow was the funeral. He'd likely not have time to make any more inquiries.

He moved back to the house as an additional weight settled in his chest.

Walter fixated on the nearby headstone, scowling as the vicar quoted the Bible, offering little comfort. A tidy crowd surrounded him, Henrietta, and his mother. Many of them had approached him before the service began, offering their sympathy and condolences. He wasn't sure what to do. It wouldn't bring Daniel back or lessen the blow of his loss. He heard the constant mutterings, the repeated phrases.

"Gone too soon."

"He was so young."

Walter hadn't bothered to search the crowd for Patience. He told himself he didn't care if she was here. If she were, she only showed her support for his brother and family.

Henrietta sobbed quietly into his shoulder. His mother stared with empty eyes at Daniel's casket, poised to be lowered into his eternal rest. It would have pained Daniel to see his family so dismal. He had his flaws, but Daniel never liked to see his family unhappy. He had been the rock after their father left this world.

Now that responsibility fell to Walter... and he wasn't sure if he was up to the task.

The vicar's sermon ended. His brother's casket lowered into the earth. Watching it descend twisted Walter's insides into an unsteady resolve. His brother would forever remain under the ground, never to resurface. Emotion caught in his throat, but he refused to let it show. His family needed him strong.

The vicar invited the family to say their last goodbyes and the vicar's wife handed Walter and each family member a rose. He stood at the edge of the grave, his sister on one arm, his mother on the other and they stared down at the gaping hole which held Daniel.

His mother gently kissed the top of her rose, then let it fall. It landed softly on the casket and Henrietta's followed, hitting with a thud. His jaw clenched. *Goodbye, brother. May I be half the man you were.* He let his rose fall, and with it, his brother.

Neighbors and friends turned to leave as Walter fixed his gaze on familiar blue eyes. He stilled. Patience stood across the lawn, in the shade of a willow. Alone, like a statue, the black of her dress accentuated the pale pallor of her fair skin. Watching, the white of her eyes pink from crying.

He wanted to go to her, find comfort in her from what he had lost. Her standing in the distance meant she still cared. The sadness in her eyes told of her loss. Every instinct in him told him to rush to her so they might share this burden together.

Instead, he bridled his emotions and kissed the top of his mother's head.

"Return to the house. I'll be along shortly."

His mother nodded as his sister clung to her, heading for the carriage he'd rented for the occasion. As soon as they were safely inside, Walter turned to face Patience. She hadn't moved. He pulled a cloak of indifference around him like a shield. Patience might feel for his loss, but her actions repeatedly proved her inconstancy.

He walked around the laborer's filling his brother's grave, and stood tall in front of the woman who had taken up his thoughts and focus for the past few months, perhaps without even realizing it.

"Walter..." she whispered. "I'm so sorry."

Everything about her was soft, comforting. But he wouldn't be pulled in by her charms again. Not today.

"I hope you are well, Miss Hawthorn."

Her eyes fluttered in surprise before looking away. "You're angry with me still."

It wasn't a question, just a statement of fact.

With harsh breath and steel in his words, he lashed out. "I have other things to occupy my time. I do not have time to feel resentment—or any feelings—toward you." He wanted her to feel his pain.

Her brows drew together as her bottom lip trembled. "Did you not receive my letter?"

Walter remained firm and unfeeling. "I never opened it," he admitted. "I used it as kindling for my fire."

"Oh." Patience's eyes pooled, a film of tears forming. "I wish you would have read it," she whispered.

So had he.

His gut twisted. Tempted to reach for her, give some comfort, but she had done enough toying with his emotions. He didn't need to read a letter full of overdone apologies. Lord Berkshire had rejected her as she had rejected him. It was in the past, and he would keep it there to save his sanity. He couldn't do it again, love her only to have her reject him, twice. He refused to risk his heart on the fickle lady.

"You have not forgiven me," she whispered, defeat in her voice.

"You are incorrect. I've done my best to forget you." Walter tipped his hat in her direction. "I wish you health and happiness."

"Walter..." Patience stopped. The tears had escaped

the corners of her eyes. "I wish I could express how sorry I am about your brother." She straightened, squaring her shoulders. "But if this is to be the last time, we speak to each other... then I want you to know I wish you the happiest of lives. A gentleman as good as you deserves only the best."

She turned from him, her black dress rustling as she walked away, her shoulders held high. She was being strong for his sake, too much spirit to grovel. The thought made him proud, despite his best effort to keep his feelings neutral. He felt hollow inside as she retreated. Without her support, he was but a shell of the man he could be.

CHAPTER 5

PATIENCE DIDN'T BELIEVE Walter would be so cruel as to forget her, not for a moment. He was hurting from the loss of his brother and was lashing out because of his perceived betrayal.

Had he really burned the letter as he said?

It would explain everything, his actions toward her. He didn't know she had not gone against her word to him.

She had made a vow when they had failed to gain permission from her parents. She would find a way to be with him. She had naively thought it would be easy to sneak away from her mother and steal moments alone with Walter. But she had miscalculated the sheer vastness of London, and the fact that they ran in different circles now that he was a barrister with little income and no status.

She had adamantly denied Walter's insistence that she would soon find another to claim her heart. He let her go with his last kiss, freeing her from any obligation to him.

The tables had turned. She had been constant in her affection, while it seemed he held resentment toward her for supposedly doing the very thing he wished her happy to do.

She determined to prove to him she still cared deeply, and that she had been as constant as the stars. He was stubborn, but so was she. She had let her mother control her life long enough. If she continued in this manner, she would turn into a shell of the person she was, as her father had already done.

Attending the funeral yesterday had been difficult, but it strengthened her in a way she had not been expecting. She no longer feared Walter's rejection. Though his words said otherwise, she knew by the stiffness of his posture and the anger in his eyes that he still cared for her deeply. Pain changed people, and she would not let Walter be changed for the worse without attempting to soothe him. She owed him that at least since it was her shameless trick that had caused the pain.

She wandered the village, strolling past a small dress shop and bakery, letting her mind wander. How was she to fix the mess she'd made of their hearts?

She had already decided she would solve the

mystery of the broken carriage. She enjoyed mysteries —it reminded her of her youth with Walter. If she could discover what caused the carriage to malfunction, perhaps Walter would appreciate her efforts and consider forgiving her.

Perhaps.

It was worth a try.

Patience made her way down the street until she reached the blacksmith's shop. She had inquired after the funeral with Walter's groom as to the whereabouts of the carriage when the family was inside mourning with a few close neighbors. She hoped it hadn't been scrapped.

She entered the shop, feeling the sweltering heat, inhaling the scent of iron and sweat.

"Miss Hawthorn! To what do I owe the pleasure?" Mr. Tate greeted her in the entryway.

Mr. Tate's round, balding head and missing teeth did not distract from the kindness he emanated. His friendly demeanor had made him a favorite amongst the village. She smiled, knowing he would not deny her request.

"I was wondering perhaps if you were in possession of the carriage Mr. Daniel Longman drove before the accident?"

"I am." Mr. Tate's brows furrowed.

Patience's spirits brightened. "Could I see it?"

Mr. Tate shrugged. "I don't see the harm in it. I was

going to strip it for scrap, but Mr. Walter Longman sent me a letter asking me not to touch it until he had inspected it. I imagine he suspects faulty manufacturing."

"Indeed." Patience followed Mr. Tate toward the back of his shop, avoiding the dingy scraps of iron that littered the floor.

A fresh breeze filtered through the open window, bringing with it the scent of horses and flowers along with a welcome breeze and light.

"Here we are. Not much to look at." Mr. Tate pointed to the pile.

Patience stopped, her eyes widening at the mess in front of her. She had not imagined so much destruction. The object in front of her hardly looked as if it had once been a carriage. It lay crumpled on its side, missing too many pieces. The top was caved in and mangled. She forced herself not to think about Daniel's crushed body trapped inside it.

"What do you think happened?" she asked in a whisper.

Mr. Tate scratched at his jaw. "I reckon something was faulty, but I haven't had the chance to examine the pieces to know if that is true. It'll be hard to narrow down exactly what caused the accident now that the carriage is in shambles."

Patience stepped closer, examining the carriage. It

was a mess, indeed. She didn't know where to start looking for clues. Had the wheel fallen off before or after the tumble? Was the underside of the carriage that bent out of shape before?

She straightened, disheartened at the lack of information it gave her.

"Thank you, Mr. Tate," she said, turning to him. "I trust you'll examine the carriage for defects that might have resulted in the accident?"

Mr. Tate nodded. "It's certainly intriguing."

He escorted Patience to the front, nearly colliding with a man entering as she exited.

"Oh!" she gasped.

"Pardon me!" the gentleman muttered, grasping her arm to steady her.

She looked up, catching Walter's surprised expression. "Patience. What are you doing here?"

She stumbled back, blinking. "I... I wanted to see the carriage." She straightened, trying to show more confidence. "I wanted to discover the cause of the accident."

To her surprise, Walter grabbed her upper arm and pulled her away from the blacksmith, dragging her behind a merchant's building before facing her with a scowl, placing both hands on her shoulders, as if she would run away.

"Miss Hawthorn," his voice low, "I do not appreciate you meddling in my private affairs."

Patience shrugged his hands away, returning his scowl. "I'm not trying to meddle. I only wanted to help."

Walter growled under his breath. "Let me handle this. Besides, I highly

your parents would approve."

Patience winced at the venom in his voice. It was unfair to bring up her parents. If her mother knew she was here, snooping into Daniel's death… "I don't let my parents control every aspect of my life," she snapped. "If I want to see you, I shall. Just as I always have."

She watched as Walter shook his head. Bowing quickly, he turned to walk away.

She caught his arm, turning him back. "You may have forgotten me, Walter Longman, but this hasn't been as easy for me either. Not a day goes by that I don't think of you." She searched his face, trying to find some tenderness in his stern gaze.

"Tell me you think of me. Tell me I don't suffer alone."

Walter stared at her in silence as she held her breath.

Finally, he sighed, looking away. "I've tried to forget you, Patience," he whispered. "Tried and failed so many times I've nearly driven myself mad. But I still harbor resentment that you paired up with a new earl only months after your parents denied me. You've lost my respect, and I'm uncertain how to capture it again. Even if I wanted to move forward in a relationship, I could not in good conscience until I can learn to trust you."

Patience let her lips part at his words. The pain she felt stirred her anger towards this silly misunderstanding.

"Perhaps if you had read my letter, you would know the reasons behind my fake courtship with Lord Berkshire," she said.

Walter opened his mouth to reply, but his breath caught. She watched him struggle.

"Fake?" he whispered.

"Yes! You insufferable lout! As if I could be so inconstant in my affection toward you. It had only been a year! You think I could not stand the temptations of society for a measly season?"

"Then why did I see you in the arms of Lord Berkshire? Why the scandal when he turned his affections to another? I wanted to throttle the both of you for your lack of discreteness and propriety!"

Patience took a step closer, only a breath apart.

"Walter, please. Let me tell you my side of the story. Then perhaps you'll understand that I never meant you any harm."

Walter's rich eyes flickered from her eyes to her

nose, her hair to her lips. His body relaxed, and his eyes softened as he looked at her.

Patience pulled in a deep breath. "Lord Berkshire and I—"

"Oh, Mr. Longman, there you are!" a voice called from behind.

Patience clamped her mouth shut, stepping away to a respectable distance. Mr. Scott, owner of the general mercantile, approached.

"I haven't seen you since the funeral. Your brother ordered a piece of jewelry for your mother but was unable to pick it up before his—" The man stopped mid-sentence, probably only now realizing the awkwardness of the situation. "Would you care to look at it?" Hope danced in his eyes.

Walter turned back to Patience and gave a quick bow.

She curtsied, lowering her voice. "Meet me at the factory when you have finished here. You know the place." She nodded.

Walter hesitated before nodding.

Patience stood alone, resting her back against the brick building, watching as the pair rounded the corner, disappearing from sight. She allowed herself to feel hope that she might earn Walter's forgiveness. He needed to settle his affairs without her watchful eye.

CHAPTER 6

THE SMALL EMERALD earrings sparkled as Mr. Scott held them up for Walter to examine. Even to Walter's undiscerning eye, he could tell they were fake.

Mr. Scott's eyes glimmered as he watched for Walter's reaction. He wasn't sure if this man was being deceitful or if he truly did not have a clue as to their authenticity. The fact that his brother had ordered them at all irritated Walter. Mr. Scott had to know Daniel's spending was out of control.

"Exquisite, aren't they?"

Walter took them, weighing the lightness in his palm. He paused, wondering how to best handle the situation. Who knew how much debt Daniel had amassed with this man? Walter needed to keep Mr. Scott happy, at least for now.

He looked up at Mr. Scott. "How much?" No matter

the cost, Walter knew he couldn't in good conscience spend any more money.

Mr. Scott grinned. "Because of the unfortunate death in your family, I'll offer half price. Three pounds."

Walter nearly dropped the earrings in his haste to extract himself from the small confines of the shop, but knew he needed to leave gently. His family's financial situation gripped his chest like a vise, and he wasn't sure if all his accounts with this man had been settled.

"I'm sorry." He handed them back to the merchant. "Not at this time."

He would not give the dreadful things to his mother even if he had a mind to, and he could not believe Daniel would have either.

Mr. Scott's face fell. "Well, perhaps these can tempt you…" He ducked behind his counter and pulled out a pair of pearl earrings. They were simple but elegant. Mr. Scott placed them in Walter's hand. Walter tried to mask his irritation as he reluctantly took the earrings.

"A gift," he said with a smile. "Give your family my condolences."

Walter curled his fingers over the earrings. "I can't take these." He extracted a few coins from his pocket and handed it to Mr. Scott.

The jeweler hesitated for a brief moment. "You are too kind," he said.

Walter placed the earrings on the counter, but the

man shoved the earrings back at him. He didn't have the strength to protest any further. He forced them in his pocket before walking out of the shop, more wound up than when he'd left his home that morning. This day was not going as he'd expected.

He was tempted to leave Patience where she was and go about his business without her interference, but couldn't bring himself to leave her alone when she expected him. He shook his head, not believing that he still hadn't learned how to put Patience behind him.

He walked to the edge of his property where an old abandoned candle factory sat alone and untouched by time. The smell of tallow assailed him as he stepped into a small room. A thin, waxy film coated the bare floors. This was where he and Patience would meet in secret when their relationship turned from friendship to love. Before he asked for her hand in marriage. He pressed forward, determined to have this meeting done with. He didn't need to relive these memories.

He walked further into the dim factory, lit only by the light spilling from its windows. Patience stepped out of the shadows, looking as if a beautiful ghost in a cream-colored dress. Walter stood still as he caught sight of her, afraid he would cave into an irrational mess if he drew nearer.

Patience fiddled with the fabric of her skirt. "It was all for you, you know," she said.

Walter's heart twisted, thumping faster at the sound of her voice, but remained stoic, not saying a word.

She continued. "Mama was pushing me at any gentleman with a title and a decent income attached to his name. I didn't want to court any of them. I was still yours."

Walter's heart beat loudly in his ears. Still, he said nothing.

"When I saw Juliana Gibbon interact with Lord Berkshire, I knew without a doubt, they were in love with each other, even if they hadn't realized it. As you probably know, he had just acquired his father's title and a sizable fortune at the passing of his father. The mothers clamored for introductions," she stepped closer. The red highlights of her hair masked in the dark shadows. "Juliana knew I didn't want to court anyone. She knew there was only one man who held my affections. So she devised a plan." Patience shrugged her shoulders as if what she had done had been a mere game to pass the time.

"She asked you to court Lord Berkshire," Walter said, guessing at the story.

She nodded as her head bent. The vise constricting his heart since he found her in the arms of Lord Berkshire loosened.

He stepped closer, unable to resist her pull. He

checked himself in time, guarding his feelings. Too many things to take into consideration.

"Society takes courtship seriously, Patience. How do you think it looked to me?"

"By pretending to court, it saved Lord Berkshire from the overzealous matrons, and I had a respite from my mother. It was all for you, Walter. You must believe that," her eyes pleaded.

His hands tightened into fists, his mind warring with his heart. "Why did the papers report it as a scandal?"

Patience huffed out a breath. "Once Lord Berkshire told my parents he had no intention of making me an offer, they pulled me out of London and brought me back home. Of course, it looked suspicious. But I swear to you—nothing occurred between Lord Berkshire and I. Lord Berkshire and Juliana are to be wed in a week's time. They have their happy ending. Why can't we have ours?" her voice softened.

Walter slipped his hand through his hair, trying to make sense of what she said. They stood in silence for a moment before he took the remaining steps towards her. "Do you still love me?"

"You know I do." Patience's eyes locked with his.

His insides danced at their proximity.

A stray lock of hair fell from her bun. He wanted to tuck it behind her ear. He wanted to touch her face. He wanted to kiss her forehead…

She breathed, "I've vowed to never marry another."

He fought not to lose control.

Her words pierced through his rough exterior, softening his heart. He reached for her, tucking her hand lightly into his. He yearned to fold her into his arms, hold her tight against his chest and promise to never let her go.

"Have you your mother's blessing?" he asked quietly.

Her eyes grew distant. "Mama does not understand me. Papa does a little, but he's too afraid to stand up for me." She lowered her gaze. "I do not have their blessing."

Walter lowered his hand, dropping hers. "Then what are we doing here, Patience?" his voice strained. "Why prolong the pain when this cannot be?"

"Because I will not give up." She lifted her chin, showing him signs of her earlier self. "There has to be a reason besides money that she won't approve of the match. I know there is." A small smile lit her face. "It's a mystery only we can solve."

Walter fought a smile. "Come now. We are no longer children."

"Don't you remember the fun we had?" Her smile, warm and genuine. "Romping around the village of Wallingford, solving the dullest mysteries we could find?"

He did. They had gotten into some mischief with their sleuthing games. It was the primary reason he pursued a career as a barrister.

"Mama's aversion to you is no different," Patience continued. "But we will crack the case. What do you say?"

Walter looked into her hopeful, optimistic face. He almost agreed, but remembered that his other responsibilities took priority. The Vanderbilt case. His brother's accident. What to do about the debts.

"I'm sorry," he said, shaking his head. "I must investigate my brother's accident first and foremost. And then… I must return to London."

Patience's face fell. "When?"

"As soon as possible. Within a week, I hope."

Patience's forehead creased. "You mean, you aren't staying in Wallingford?"

"I can't." Walter took a step back, distancing himself from her. This would not end well. Her mother would never agree. He still worked, something Mrs. Hawthorn didn't understand.

Gentlemen didn't work.

No matter how they felt for each other… he had responsibilities to care for his family. "I have to take on a case in London. It is career-defining. And…" He hesitated, then plowed on. "My brother left my family heavily indebted. I have no choice but to return to

London and make my way as a barrister. Hopefully, I'll pay off some debts in a few years if the bank will agree. My brother mortgaged the estate and I don't want to lose my mother's home."

Patience's eyes searched his. He looked away for fear she'd see how hard this was for him. Giving in to his heart would only create more problems.

"Take me with you." Her quiet pleading forced his eyes back to hers.

He shook his head. "I can't. Not without your parents' blessing."

"Do you still love me?"

His eyes found Patience's. They were wide, uncertain. Something inside broke, and he loathed himself for causing her pain.

"I do," he whispered. "I never stopped."

Color returned to her cheeks as she reached for him. He drew back, fighting everything within him that wanted to touch and hold her.

She dropped her hands, bunching them at her sides.

"I will help you find out about your brother's accident," she said firmly. "And then, before you return to London, we will approach my parents."

Walter shook his head. "Patience, leave my brother's accident to me. I will get to the bottom of it soon enough. As for your parents…" He paused, shaking his head. "Believe me, I want to ask them again for your hand. But I know they'll give the same answer they did last time, and I cannot bear to go through the humiliation again." He took a deep breath. "Now is not the right time."

Patience's gaze fell to the wax-smeared ground. "I understand," she said quietly.

Walter hesitated, then carefully extended his hand, lifting her chin until she looked at him again. "I haven't given up on us," he breathed. "But it'll have to wait. At least, until I've won the case in London. By then, I'll be making the money to give you a home. I'll be more desirable to your family."

He moved his hand to her cheek, slipping his fingers along her jaw, stroking her smooth skin with his thumb. "Don't give up on me. I will come for you."

Patience nodded, though still looking disappointed. Walter hated disappointing her.

He released her, stepping away. "Stay out of trouble until I bring you word." A smile cracked his lips.

Her eyes filled with hope, making it difficult to leave. Taking a breath, he turned and left the building, leaving things partially mended between them. He hoped it was enough, though something inside him knew their relationship wouldn't mend so easily.

CHAPTER 7

THE DAY WAS HALF-GONE, but it had been worth it to see Patience again. His step felt lighter as he weaved his way through the streets, heading straight for the blacksmith. Though his brother had only been in the ground for a full day, speaking with Patience had lifted his spirits. His heart was heavy, but knowing the woman he loved knew his struggles, lifted it slightly. There was no way he could tell his mother about the debts. He had no idea how she would take the news, believing Daniel had been a good provider. And though he knew Patience couldn't be of use to him, the thought of her constancy buoyed him. He'd been wrong to distrust her.

With the funeral still fresh in his mind, he determined to find answers. His gut told him his brother's death was not an accident.

Mr. Tate greeted him with a toothless grin as he

entered the blacksmith's shop. The only blacksmith in Wallingford, he'd known Mr. Tate since he was a boy.

"Ah, there you are! Was wondering when you'd be coming around."

Walter nodded. "The carriage?"

Mr. Tate turned to move into the back of the shop. "Right this way, sir."

Walter followed the blacksmith as he led him to the back. Lifting a lantern, Walter spotted the mangled metal that had once been a carriage. His stomach lurched at the gruesome sight, one that sent his imagination turning at how his brother could have died. Suffocation, broken bones, cracked skull, punctured lungs… the list of possibilities ran through his mind.

Mr. Tate handed him the lantern as he approached the destroyed carriage. Kneeling, Walter examined the bent and twisted metal. "How could this have happened?" he asked quietly.

Mr. Tate shuffled his feet beside him. "There most certainly could have been a weakness in the metal the manufacturer used. Perhaps it just snapped after the wheel came off."

Walter scowled at the mess in front of him. "But where? What could have broken that would have thrown the carriage completely off the road?"

Mr. Tate hunched next to Walter. "Let's see… well,

the horses escaped, yes? That should give us some clues."

Walter nodded. "Perhaps they spooked and broke free—something they'd only be able to do if the carriage shaft snapped." He lifted his eyes to the carriage's front. The metal that would loop through the horse's tethers had indeed broken off.

Mr. Tate ran his fingers along the thin metal, shaking his head. "No, no... they broke away after the carriage lost control. See here—" The blacksmith tapped where the metal had broken. "It's twisted, bent. Whatever happened, the force was enough that the metal twisted right off, freeing the horses."

Walter's brow knit. "But they are securely tied. What could have possibly caused the carriage to swerve one way and the horses the other?"

Mr. Tate lowered his eyes, studying the mess, scratching the back of his neck. "The way this metal broke... I'd almost say the carriage collapsed downward..." He imitated with his hands, leveling them beside each other, then violently dropping one hand. "And caused the metal bars to snap up, giving them an enormous amount of stress. Any carriage of this make would have the front snapped off if this was the case."

Walter contemplated what Mr. Tate was saying. "Then... if a wheel dislodged, would that have dropped the carriage enough to break off the front?"

Mr. Tate ducked his head to examine the underside of the carriage. "If one wheel fell off, that certainly could have done it. But the wheel didn't simply fall off —the metal it was attached to is gone, too." He pointed. "Ah-ha. The axle snapped in half."

A chill ran through Walter. "Snapped in half? What would that have done to the carriage?"

"The front wheels' axle is what snapped, so it would have dropped dramatically forward." Mr. Tate once again imitated with his hand, slanting one at an angle. "It would have certainly broken the carriage shaft, freeing the horses. But now the wheels are not able to function properly, and depending on how fast your brother was going, it most certainly would have pitched him forward or to the side."

Walter stood, straightening. "And then what?"

Mr. Tate shrugged. "It seems to have rolled onto its side. Mr. Longman was found in a ravine with the carriage. It must have pitched to the side, losing one of the wheels, and tumbled down the hill with him on it. The force of the fall could have certainly crushed him."

Walter felt sick to his stomach. "The manufacturer is at fault then?" he asked, his anger heightening.

Mr. Tate took a moment to examine the fractured axle. "No," he said slowly. "No... I... That's strange."

Walter peered at the axle, trying to discern it all. "What is it?"

Mr. Tate squinted. "The axle didn't snap from poorly made metal," he said. "I've seen fractured metal before. No... this was deliberately cut. Right here." He pointed. "But not all the way, of course. This tiny bit here—" he pointed to the bottom bit of the metal rod. "That broke from all the pressure." Mr. Tate's eyes moved slowly to Walter. His tone somber. "Mr. Longman. It appears someone meant harm to your brother."

Mr. Tate's words pounded into Walter. He stared at the severed axle, trying to piece it all together. "You're sure? I don't know anyone who would do such a thing."

"You can see the marks right here, sir," Mr. Tate pointed.

Walter's anger deepened as he spotted the jagged marks of a file that had been dragged through the metal, just enough to weaken it.

He moved back out from the wreckage and stood, his head spinning. "Thank you, Mr. Tate," he said hoarsely as he walked out of the shop, the world around him crumbling into a cold abyss.

Someone murdered his brother.

He didn't remember the return home as he moved through the front entrance. Henrietta was playing somber songs on the pianoforte. The plodding melody seemed darker than before as he thought of Daniel's premature death.

He retreated to his study, shutting the door behind

him, blocking out the music. He leaned his back against the door for several minutes, staring at the desk his brother had occupied only a week ago.

Daniel was murdered. The dreadful thought forming in his head. Who would murder his brother?

Walter flinched at the thought of anyone wishing that kind of harm to his brother. He could think of no one who would have done it or wished him dead.

He found the strength to move to the desk where a new stack of letters awaited him. Walter found a letter opener and methodically began slicing them open one by one. Would he find a clue in Daniel's correspondence?

The first was from Mr. Welch. As promised, he had sent new details of the Vanderbilt case. He hinted that Walter should be there no later than next Friday—giving him only a week to finish sorting through Daniel's mess of affairs. One week to investigate Daniel's murder.

Shuddering, Walter tucked Mr. Welch's letter into his pocket so he might study the new case details later that evening.

He opened the second letter—an invoice from the wine merchant. Walter stared at the requested amount, his mind blanking. Who spent such an exorbitant amount on wine? Someone who wanted to drown the world out. Someone who was frightened. Did Daniel suspect ill will toward him?

Walter set aside the invoice and opened another letter. Another invoice, this one from the tailor. The payment was long overdue. He shoved aside the rest of the letters, refusing to open another. Leaning his elbows on the desk, he dug his fingers into his hair, closing his eyes.

Daniel had been murdered. He couldn't get the thought from his head.

What was the motive? Had his brother been foolish enough to get into debt with dangerous men? Walter opened his eyes and gazed at the pile of bills again. The way he'd been spending money, it wouldn't surprise him.

"Daniel, what have you done?" Walter murmured, rubbing at his eyes.

Walter straightened in his chair, a sudden fire in his gut. He only had a week before he would return to London. He'd be hanged if he spent it wallowing in questions, not actively searching for answers. The first thing he needed to do was cut expenses.

Immediately.

He pulled out a pack of financial records and once again began shuffling through them, making a pile of expenses that were necessary and a pile they could do without. He had no choice but to talk with his mother tomorrow about the situation, but he'd come up with a plan to resolve things first.

He caught notice of recent additions to the household servants as he filed through the accounts. Walter's brows furrowed, thinking it reckless to hire on additional help when they already couldn't afford to keep on those they had. Daniel had hired two new servants—a groom and house maid.

Walter ignited in confusion and frustration. Why did Daniel feel the need to hire a second man when Benjamin was more than capable of handling four horses on his own? He made a note to let the new groomsman go today. The only useful thing he had likely managed was helping haul the mangled carriage to the blacksmith.

Walter froze, staring at the document, his vision losing focus.

Two men had been around to prepare Daniel's carriage. One of them must have noticed suspicious behavior... or worse.

Darting to his feet, Walter rushed out the study door, nearly trampling his mother who stood in the corridor.

"Walter!" his mother looked him up and down. "Are you well? You look flushed."

Walter gave her a quick kiss on the forehead. He couldn't tell her about his recent discoveries. Not yet.

"I've some urgent business to attend to," he said, as he stuck a hand in his pocket, feeling the pearl earrings he'd forgotten.

He shuffled his feet nervously, wondering what he should do with them. A last gift from his brother might be a comfort to her.

"I have a gift from Daniel." He drew out the earrings and presented them to her, noting her reaction.

His mother's face fell as she studied the earrings.

"Oh, Walter... they're beautiful, but Daniel has given me too much already. And frankly—" She paused, offering a sweet smile, one that Walter tried and failed to return. "I fear we cannot afford such extravagance," her eyes held concern.

He nodded to her, grateful she seemed to grasp the trouble they were in.

"I am looking into the accounts and am doing my best to keep us above water."

His mother seemed to relax, and he was glad he had not talked to her sooner about the situation. If things became worse, he would inform her of their predicament, but only if he must.

Daniel had fallen for Mr. Scott's schemes over and over again, it seemed, and he was beginning to wonder about Daniel's true capacity to run the house properly.

He gave her another quick kiss before leaving for the stables. He found Benjamin sitting in the afternoon sun. The old groom moved to his feet as Walter approached.

"Good day to you, sir," he said. "How can I be of assistance?"

"Is the groom Daniel hired a month ago here?"

Benjamin nodded. "In with the horses," he nodded toward a stall. "We've been taking turns, switching duties every other day," he grinned. "We have treated your horses like kings since they hired George."

Walter thanked Benjamin, trying to wipe the scowl off his face as he entered the stable where George was brushing Apollo.

The new boy bowed as Walter walked in, not uttering a word.

Walter eyed the boy. He was young—perhaps not fifteen. Dark hair slicked back, revealing dark eyes. The young man averted his gaze, his focus on brushing the horse.

"I understand you are the new hire," Walter said.

"Yes, sir."

"Were you the one who hitched the carriage the day my brother died?"

The boy hesitated. "Yes, sir."

Walter picked his next words carefully. "Is there anything I should know? Have you seen any suspicious characters around?"

The groom's brows pulled together. "Sir?"

Walter stared hard at the young man, gauging his body language, the flicker of his eyes. "My brother's carriage failed a week ago. I have reason to suspect foul play. Someone has tampered with the carriage. It may have been the day my brother took it out. Would you know anything of it?"

The groom shook his head, his eyes wide. "No, sir. Honest, sir, I've seen only Benjamin and myself."

Walter grit his teeth. "What's your name?"

"George, sir."

"How is it you came across this job, George?"

George absently ran a hand along the stallion's chestnut coat. "I applied to the house, sir. My family needed the income. I had good references. Mr. Longman said he liked my character well enough. Said if Apollo liked me, so did he."

Walter examined the stallion before turning his eyes back to the young groom.

"You're sure you didn't see anything strange just before my brother's death?"

"No, sir," George paused. His hand frozen on Apollo's flank. "Only… I caught a maid and the groundskeeper in the stable the night before."

Walter's stomach churned. "Did you?"

"Yes. They were…" George shuffled his feet uncomfortably. "Quite friendly with each other, sir."

Walter sighed. There wasn't anything suspicious about that, he supposed. Still, he asked George for a description of the maid—short, with mousy hair. Walter felt satisfied that he had gleaned all he could from the young man.

Walter suddenly felt tired, but didn't want to return to the house to be reminded of his brother's death, the mountain of debt hanging over the household, and his sister's morose music.

He looked at Apollo, his fists tightening. "George, would you saddle the stallion?" He needed a good, hard ride to clear his mind.

Within the hour, he was on Apollo's back, feeling some control again. He pushed the horse faster, giving Apollo his head, galloping over the estate, veering east —toward the Hawthorn house.

As he passed, his thoughts turned to Patience and to her mother, who hated him because he was a working gentleman. Did Mrs. Hawthorn even consider him a gentleman, now that he worked for his living? Did he dare bring Patience into a household so burdened with debt?

He galloped, letting the scenery blur into oblivion. How had his life become so tangled in such a short time? And how was he ever to get out of it?

CHAPTER 8

PATIENCE COULD NO LONGER sit around the house, worrying about how Walter was faring, especially after finding out about his brother's debts and the pressure he was under to get back to his case in London. Though it hurt to lose him so soon after their misunderstandings were resolved, the knowledge he still loved her gave her hope.

She set out for a walk even though it felt like rain. She looked up at the gray sky, tasting the humid air. The wind whipped at her hair as her feet carried her past the gardens, the stables, and over the hill near her parents' property. She found the familiar dirt road that took her to the edge of the Longman estate. A mile and a half later, she came across the familiar cropping of trees and the low stone wall that marked the Longman's property.

She hesitated, looking past the wall and at the

estate's fields, golden with dry wheat ready to harvest. Cattle and sheep dotted the rolling hills while thunder rumbled above her. Her mind made up, she sat on the waist-high stone wall. Lifting her skirts, she swung her legs over. She continued on her journey across the estate's lands, breathing in the scent of wet earth and listening to the twittering of birds looking for their own shelter.

Her excursion wasn't purely out of curiosity. She had stayed up long into the night, thinking about the mangled carriage. Walter had said he wanted to discover why the carriage had failed, killing his brother. She wondered if perhaps anyone nearby knew any details they might keep from him.

If Mrs. Longman found her — Patience put the thought from her mind. She liked Walter's mother and believed the lady was fond of her, despite her own mother.

Henrietta, his sister, was the kindest person in Wallingford. Though things had been awkward between the three of them since Patience's mother had refused Walter. Patience had only conversed once with them after their fallout, and that was only because she'd run into them in town.

The Longmans no longer invited her to their estate for social gatherings, and her mother continued to exclude the Longmans from her own picnics and parties.

Patience didn't understand why her mother had never connected with them. It was unusual for influential families in the same neighborhood to be so distant.

Patience felt the squish of earth beneath her feet. Mud covered her boots as she stepped into the soft earth. She continued to pick her way across the grassy field. Grazing cattle lifted their heads, watching as she passed. The first light raindrops tickled her nose, wetting her cheekbones. She crested a hill and spotted a farmer's cottage. Beyond that, she could just make out the top of Walter's house, dipping past another green hill. She walked forward, planning to talk with the stable hands, inquiring about the state of the carriage before it had wrecked.

Five steps later, thunder clapped, opening the sky as pouring rain dropped onto the countryside. Lifting her arms over her head, she tried to keep the rain from her eyes. By the time she made it to the stables, she would be utterly soaked. But turning toward home would be just as miserable.

She licked her lips, tasting the chilly rain. She could see a cottage in the distance where she could seek shelter until the rain passed.

Patience lifted her skirts and ran, her boots squelching in the mud. She felt her curls coming loose from her bonnet, but she ignored it, focusing on getting to the cottage before she was completely drenched.

Arriving at the doorstep nearly soaked through, she knocked and waited, pushing her wet hair out of her eyes. A curtain moved in the window as someone peered out. Within moments, the door flung wide. Before she could speak, a short, round woman was pulling her inside.

"My dear, what are you doing out in this weather?" She looked her up and down. "You'll catch your death."

Patience took a moment to catch her breath. "I'm sorry. I was just passing by and... thank you for letting me inside. I didn't expect such a downpour."

The woman clucked her tongue. "Let me get you a towel to dry yourself." The woman's eyes shot downward. "Look at the *state* of your shoes!"

Patience stood by the doorway as the woman whisked away to the kitchen for the towel. A light rustling sounded to Patience's right, and she looked around to see two small girls peeking out from a room. They disappeared, giggling when she caught sight of them.

The woman returned, waving a threadbare towel. "Here," she said, handing it to Patience. "Clean up as best you can."

"Thank you." She sopped her hair, squeezing it between her fingers while looking about the cottage. It was a cozy space, with a kitchen, dining area, and two bedrooms.

"I'm Patience Hawthorn. May I ask your name?" If the woman recognized her name, she didn't show it.

"Marcy Brown," she said. "My husband is Jeremy Brown. He's out tending to the pigs, I believe. He'd better be in the barn, or that man will go to an early grave."

Patience smiled, glancing toward the bedroom where the young girls had disappeared. "And you have children?"

"Yes, Lily and Rose." Mrs. Brown smiled. "Go ahead and remove your shoes. I just cleaned the floors this week."

Patience obeyed, unlacing her boots and sliding them off. Thankfully, her stockings were still dry. She moved further into the cottage as Mrs. Brown offered her a seat at the dining room table.

"You're on the Longman estate, you know," Mrs. Brown said.

"Yes. I am a… friend of Walter Longman."

Mrs. Brown shook her head. "Poor boy. Making his way in London and then called back home over the tragic death. Now he'll have all those debts to worry about."

Patience froze, freshly seated. "Debts?" How was this woman so acquainted with Walter's personal business?

Mrs. Brown sat across from her. "We've heard all

the gossip around town. Seems his accounts are overdue," she said in a low voice, almost distraught. "It only makes sense that they can't afford to keep up the estate much longer."

Patience couldn't believe Walter's family business was known so widely throughout the village. Did her mother know? Maybe this was why she'd been so obstinate in her refusal of Walter. Perhaps she thought him a fortune hunter.

She tried to tell herself it wasn't her concern. And yet, it was. Her mother knew their feelings toward each other. Knew they had been inseparable since their youth. Walter was not after her parents' money.

"It's been hard on us," Mrs. Brown continued. "We lived comfortably enough with our farm, but now that the estate is in trouble, we're unsure if a new owner will be as good to us. The rents are low here, and we're established. There's no telling what a new owner will do. He puts us all at risk with the few families lucky enough to live on his land." She shook her head as she glanced back at the room where the girls were hiding. "I'm worried for our children. This farm has always been our home."

New owners? Would Walter have to sell the estate? Her heart flipped. This would make matters worse with her mother. How would she ever consent to their marriage if Walter was forced to sell the estate?

Patience felt for the woman and her family. "I'm sorry to hear it. I can tell Mr. Longman of your concerns. I know him to be generous and caring," she said, her voice soft. She thought of her own family, who had more than enough to help Walter if they joined their families. "I don't live far, and we've been close friends our whole lives. He'll understand your fear."

"Bless you, child," Mrs. Brown said. "I wouldn't want to burden you."

Patience shook her head. "No burden at all."

She remained with Mrs. Brown, helping her wash dishes and knead bread while they waited for the storm to pass. Lily and Rose crept from their room, helping knead the dough, giggling and laughing at Patience's lack of skill. Mrs. Brown frowned at her daughters and showed Patience how it was done.

The rain passed as suddenly as it began and Patience left, having gained new friends, and promised to talk with Walter of the tenants' concerns with a new resolve to help. She wasn't ready to return home, her mind was full of Walter and his brother's death. She would help him, feeling a little hurt that he wouldn't trust her help.

Had he learned anything from the blacksmith? If she was going to help solve the mystery, she needed to know everything he did.

Strengthening her resolve, Patience cut back toward town, knowing she looked a mess from the earlier rain.

She avoided the puddles, but the mud was unavoidable in places. Lifting her skirts, she trudged on. Her mother would be angry if she ruined this dress.

Her boots were caked with the wet earth by the time she reached the blacksmith. Not caring what people thought, she pushed forward. She heard her name before entering Mr. Tate's place. Turning, her heart leaped into her throat as she sighted Walter striding towards her, his long coat unfurling around his legs, his face grim. He didn't say a word as he reached her and took her arm, pulling her away from the blacksmith's.

"What are you doing here?" he asked, his voice low as he continued to steer her forward down the boardwalk.

"I wanted to know what the blacksmith found about the carriage," she said, holding her head high.

He groaned. "Patience, why won't you *listen?* This is none of your concern."

"Why won't you let me help?" she demanded. "A year ago, you would have."

Walter stopped, turning to face her. She waited, her heart beating fast against her chest.

He looked away from her as his jaw clenched. "You distract me," he admitted.

She could feel her face heat as he looked back to her, his expression worn and tired. "I have too much to handle, and little time. I can't focus on the task at hand with you snooping around distracting me. It's best if you keep away. Just until I get things sorted."

Patience's lips parted as she tried to come up with a response. She relaxed. It felt good to know she was a distraction, a pleasant distraction she hoped.

"Two heads are better than one," she reminded him. "I could help you. Please let me try." Her heart yearned to be close to him. To help him overcome this trial. Recently he would have let her and been happy about it. She didn't like that her actions strained their relationship.

Walter shook his head. But she refused to let it drop. She needed to get through to him. If she didn't, she feared she would lose his trust forever.

She took his hand, not caring who witnessed it. "I will not give up on you," she said fiercely. "You know of my feelings for you. Please let me help."

He didn't respond, so she pressed on.

"I already know your financial situation," she whispered. "I spoke with the Browns. They are worried about the stability of the estate. The entire village knows of your financial struggles, and your tenants are worried they will lose everything if the estate is sold. Walter, you must help them."

Walter's eyes grew sharp. "Have you been snooping into my affairs?"

"Certainly not." She felt affronted. "Mrs. Brown

gave me shelter during the rain. She told me of the village gossip and her concern for the estate."

Walter let out a breath. His features softened, though she could see the stress behind his eyes. He looked at her for the first time, taking in her limp hair and muddied hem. He shook his head, a low laugh escaping his lips.

"You really don't give up, do you?" A smile played about his tired lips.

Lips she wanted to kiss.

"Your mother will be unhappy that you've damaged your skirt."

"My maid will take it to the laundry before she finds out," Patience bit her lip. Trying to remain firm. "I'm helping you, no matter what you say. I understand that you are under a lot of stress. You need my help."

She shook her head, fighting back a smile. Was she finally getting through to him?

He ran a hand through his hair. "Yes, my brother left the estate deeply in debt, but I have no intention of selling the estate. I'm handling it now, but I've got my brother's death occupying my mind and the case I left behind in London."

"Why don't you drop the case?" Patience asked. "It will take the pressure off. Surely someone else can take over in your stead. Your brother was killed, won't they understand?"

"I can't. It will secure my career and I cannot let my mentor, Mr. Welsh, down. He has assured me I will be highly compensated and sought after if we win this case. After finding my family's estate in financial strain, I need this case more than ever."

Patience bit her bottom lip. "You must take me with you when you go."

Walter leveled her with a stern stare. "Patience, we've talked about this."

"I'm old enough to make my own decisions. I don't need my parents' blessing."

Walter shut his mouth. His face became dark, and he began to walk again, leading her toward the end of town.

"It would be my honor to walk you home, Miss Hawthorn," he said stiffly.

Patience's spirits dropped as her stomach churned. He would not let her help. Rather than fight, she followed him, trying to keep pace with him.

"You do not love me." She stopped as realization fell upon her. It was the only explanation for his change of behavior toward her.

He stopped beside her, searching her eyes.

"I do." The longing in his voice confirmed his statement.

"Then why refuse me?"

"I believe it was you who *refused me*."

Patience's mouth dropped. "My *parents* refused you. I've been trying to get you back ever since."

Walter sighed. Moving them forward again.

"You don't understand. Your parents are right. Socially and financially, we are not a good match. My family needs money. You won't have a dowry without your parents' blessing." He looked to the ground, kicking aside a stone. "I would not be able to adequately provide for you… or my mother and sister. I must find a bride whose parents will accept me."

Patience's walk slowed to a stop, and Walter turned to face her again.

For an endless moment, they stared at each other, Patience fighting back the urge to scream at his pigheadedness. She hated the stern way he looked at her —not at all like the smiles he had frequently given her. It was all wrong. Walter could not mean to give up on them so easily. There had to be a way.

He must have seen the hurt in her eyes, because he took a step toward her, then hesitated, clasping his hands behind his back. "Patience…"

She didn't respond, didn't know how, so she moved past him, putting distance between them. It was his decision. No matter how much she told him of her love, she really had no choice. For a moment, she wondered. Was it time to let him go? Her throat tightened. She pushed back the moisture stinging her eyes. She felt him rush forward catching her elbow, bringing her near. She felt a rush of adrenaline at his sudden proximity, his urgent touch.

"If you help me, you must promise to keep anything you learn hushed up. There are things I know about my brother's death that may shock you. I want you to understand that. I want you to be safe."

She nodded; breathless at his sudden turnaround. "I understand."

He leaned closer. "Meet me outside my home tomorrow morning by the stables. Do you think you can slip away?"

She nodded. Happy he'd come to his senses.

"I will tell you everything I know then, and with your help, hopefully we can find the person who... we'll find out what happened."

Patience nodded again, her head spinning. What could be so troubling about his brother's death? Why was he so secretive?

"I'll be there," she promised.

Walter released her. Then, as if a second thought accrued, he took her hand, bowed, and kissed the back of it lightly, making her insides flutter.

"Until tomorrow." Dropping her hand, he walked past her back toward town.

She stood for a moment, alone in her thoughts. Was this really happening? She had dreamed of this for so long. She could hardly believe Walter had let her back into his confidence. She would not let this opportunity pass. Before the sun set on the day tomorrow, Walter would see reason again and agree to let her into his life for good. The thought made her ecstatically happy, and she wondered if sleep would come tonight.

CHAPTER 9

WALTER WANDERED around the front of the house, unable to keep still. His sister had given up playing the pianoforte for now, for which he was grateful. But his mother still stayed locked in her rooms hating how much Daniel's death had affected her health. He had to care for and protect her and Henrietta, no matter the cost.

Walter hadn't been able to sleep much last night. He couldn't believe he had agreed to let Patience in on his investigation. But when she mentioned how he didn't have to do this alone, it struck him. He realized it would help to have a confidante, to have another mind working with him as they had done while they were young. Patience had always been one of his best and loyal friends, and had always been his first choice in sharing secrets.

He heard a noise and Patience came around the corner of the stable, just as the sun was warming the earth. Her day dress enhanced the red in her auburn hair as the morning light hit her just right. His chest constricted as she neared, a bright smile lit her face. He wanted her by his side for the rest of his life, but the impediments that stood between them were still too great.

It was only a fantasy.

After her parents' initial refusal, and now his family's debts, he couldn't rationalize offering for her again. His heart twisted in pain at the thought of giving her up, but inside he knew it was the responsible thing to do.

She approached. His jaw clenched. He would tell her what he learned from the blacksmith. It was only fitting she be the first person he told, given the place she held in his heart. But revealing the murder to another person would make it more real.

Patience smiled as she reached his side.

"I slipped out before my mother came down for breakfast. I told the groom I was going to ride to the village. I won't be missed for a few hours. Are you ready to investigate?" she asked, optimistic as a sunflower shining in the morning's light.

He wanted to partake in her optimism, and he tried

to return the smile, but feared it was more like a grimace.

"Come. I don't want my family knowing you're here, so you'll need to remain silent." He took her hand, ignoring the heat that ran through his body. He walked to the house, pulling her through the side door, leading her up the stairs to the study. All the while Patience moved silently on her tiptoes. Memories came flooding back. They'd done this too often to count, but this time the stakes were much higher.

Safely inside the study, Walter closed the door and locked it. He realized they were alone. It suddenly struck him that if they were found, Patience would be compromised. But the unconventional situation warranted it. He'd longed to be betrothed, to call her his wife, but now, no one could find them here.

Alone.

He looked at her. She was watching him, silently. He balled his fists to keep himself in check. His jaw tightened.

"We're alone," she smiled.

Did she not know how hard it was to keep from touching her when she was around?

Her brows raised as she looked around.

Tempting him like this was only making it harder for the both of them. Every instinct in him told him to go to her and give her what they both wanted. But he knew if he tasted her sweet kisses, he could never go back. He'd done it once before and it nearly broke him.

She walked slowly toward him. Her perfect brows lifted in challenge. He squeezed his fists tighter as pain shot through his palms. He wouldn't be surprised if he'd drawn blood. Pain was good. It would keep him grounded. He should back away, but he felt rooted to the spot as if he were a planet stuck in her gravity, unable to break free.

She stopped mere inches from him. Her eyes scanning each feature of his face, flitting from jawbone, to lips, to nose, to eyes—she stopped there. Her challenge vanished, turning to longing. He held his breath, waiting for her to back down, and then he saw something change in her eyes.

Determination?

She brought her hands to his face and cupped it lightly. Her touch felt wonderful on the stubble of his cheeks, though he stiffened at the slight movement while wishing her closer, wishing for more. She slowly pulled his face to hers. The action caused him to relax. To melt into her touch. A scent of rose water lingered. When had she changed her perfume? Her lips were nearly upon his. She moved her arms, encircling his waist. Her eyes trusting. It nearly undid him. He moved his lips to her ear, grasping at the last vestige of control he had.

"If I kiss you, I fear I will never stop." His pleading was but a whisper.

She let out a measured breath, nodding her acquiescence. He moved one arm around her waist while twisting his other hand through her hair. He hugged her one last time before letting her go.

She did not fight him.

He banished her touch from his mind.

They had work to do.

Patience did not look at him as she took a seat behind the desk. He sat beside her, probably too close as he scooted a chair next to her. He mulled over his next words. Patience waited, still not casting her eyes toward him, her chest rising and falling as her breathing slowed.

He straightened, clearing his throat. "The blacksmith and I discovered that Daniel's death was not an accident. Someone sawed through the axle, weakening it, causing it to snap during his journey." Walter did not so much as pause to take in air at his explanation. "Our leading suspicion is that someone wished to harm Daniel—" He paused, afraid to say the next words. "We fear he was intentionally killed."

"Murdered."

She gasped, covering her mouth with her hands, her eyes widening larger than he'd ever seen them.

"Walter," she whispered, her eyes softening as she took in the information. "I'm so sorry." Her hand flew to his, and she squeezed tightly. He grasped it, bending to place a kiss on her palm before straightening and clearing his throat.

"The next thing we need to consider is a motive."

"Do you have any ideas?" Patience whispered. As if someone was listening at the door.

Walter lifted the financial records he'd left sprawled on the desk, thinking. "I would suspect that his debts have something to do with it, but I can't be sure."

Patience followed his gaze touching a page of the records, her brows coming together in a frown.

"Have you found anything to imply he owed money to someone dangerous?"

Walter shook his head. "There are so many debts. But I haven't seen a large enough sum drawn out anywhere."

Patience bit at her bottom lip, distracting his thoughts, making him wish to taste them himself.

"Either he didn't borrow money from someone dangerous, and the recorded debts are correct," she said slowly, "or he did, and didn't record it. In which case— you're in deeper debt than you realized."

Walter waved it off. "If there's no record, I shouldn't have to worry about it. Unless someone approaches me, I'll assume everything is here. They wouldn't have killed him if he still owed them money."

Patience nodded, opening a drawer, looking up at him under her long lashes. "May I?"

He blew out a breath. He'd found nothing in the desk that would cause Daniel's murder.

"By all means." He let her do her sleuthing. She was better at it than him.

She riffled through the drawer, looking through letters and other documents. "There must be some clue in here somewhere."

Walter sidled close beside her and joined her in sifting through the drawers, pulling out anything that seemed interesting or pertinent. A handful of letters stood out, but most of the documents were bills and invoices. He didn't even know which ones had or hadn't been paid.

Patience picked up a letter, scanning it, her forehead creasing.

"Walter." She leaned into him, sliding the letter towards him.

A whiff of her scent distracted him. He focused on the words. There were glimpses of conversation.

"Haymarket Theatre? In London? Why is he corresponding with them?" His eyes dropped to the signature.

Gabriella Fox.

His eyebrows lifted. His brother was corresponding with a stage actress. The atmosphere in the room suddenly changed as the realization of what this might mean hit him.

He took the letter from Patience and scanned it, his eyes widening as he continued to read. He turned to Patience. Her cheeks had reddened. She'd read the letter too. He cleared his throat, feeling he'd stumbled upon his brother's deepest, darkest secret yet. It was littered with seductive innuendos and hopes of their future together as husband and wife. Miss Fox went on to insist he visit her soon and not to worry about his financial situation. She would keep his mind—among other things—occupied.

"It's time you return home. I'm sorry you had to see this." He folded the letter and slipped it into his waistcoat pocket. "I should have protected you from this… darkness. Please, let me figure this out alone." He stood, backing away from her.

If someone caught them here alone, they'd be forced to marry.

Patience stood and moved to his side. She looked him square in the eyes.

"I am not the innocent you left behind."

His heart constricted. What could she mean? She must have seen the uncertainty in his eyes, for she stepped closer and placed a hand on his elbow. A hard lump lodged in his throat. Was she brought so hastily back to the country because she'd been sullied, touched?

He'd kill Lord Berkshire. His eyes turned hard as he looked away.

"Walter, look at me." Her quiet pleading forced his eyes to return to hers. She gulped. "When I went to the east end of London, I saw things I wish I could banish from my mind. The filth, the desperation, the lowest of humanity, scratching and clawing to make an existence." She stopped as if trying to banish images from her mind. "I almost didn't make it out with my virtue intact. One could argue that I didn't."

That last sentence broke him. He pulled her into his arms, kissing hot tears that fell from her eyes. He trailed his kisses down her cheek in quick succession until his lips met hers. He never imagined how both wonderful and desperate her kisses could be. If he could take every pain they'd suffered in each other's absence, he would. He should have ignored her parents and taken her off to become his wife without her parents' blessing. It would have been hard, but nothing could be as hard as the separation they'd endured.

As the intensity of his emotion cooled, so did his kisses. He slowed, kissing her with more purpose, remembering the closeness they'd once shared. He pulled away, taking in her rumpled state.

"I'm sorry." He shook his head, clearing the fog,

forcing them back to reality. Her look still held sorrow as she stepped back into his arms.

He pulled her close, breathing her in once more. "You are not sullied. Even if—" His voice broke, and he cleared his throat. "Even if—you had been compromised, well and truly I mean, you would still be whole in my eyes." He paused, letting his words sink into her heart. "Know this. I would have never sent you to the east end." He squeezed tighter as a yelp escaped her lips.

He stood perfectly still, just holding her as her cries slowly calmed. She backed away, looking resolved.

"I'm sorry. We should be figuring out your brother's murder."

He shook his head. "We needed to resolve that issue first."

She nodded, and he walked back to the desk. "I will look at the rest of the letters later. Daniel was in charge of the estate. He was expected to marry a wealthy woman to bring money to the estate. With his frivolous spending, he'd especially need a rich wife. I don't understand his actions."

It infuriated Walter that Daniel would throw away his responsibilities for an actress who seemed to have little to no standards, let alone funds needed to secure the estate.

He felt Patience's breath on his neck, light and

steady. "Do you think there could be a link? Perhaps Daniel had been involved with the wrong woman and someone came after your brother for it?"

Walter frowned. "I highly doubt a man would kill for an actress," he said bitterly, thinking of the mess his brother had left behind.

His mind spun at the implications. From the sound of it, Daniel had been invested in Miss Fox. He had visited her several times. Perhaps she knew something the rest of them didn't. He turned to Patience. She still stared at him, but this time, he saw joy in her eyes. He held back his smile. "I must go straightaway to London."

Patience stood again, and Walter moved to the door. "Perhaps we should look for more clues first."

"No. If anyone knows about who might want to harm Daniel, it's this woman." He patted his breast pocket containing Daniel's letters. "I must speak to her soon, before the murderer suspects."

"Let me come with you," Patience pleaded.

Walter gave her a stern glare. "No—" He enunciated the words clearly. "I won't be gone long, just a day or two. I need to speak with my mentor about the case I'm working on as well."

"What would you like me to do while you're away then? I can't just sit idly by and do nothing."

Walter shook his head. "Stay out of trouble. I don't want you to get hurt again."

"I can take care of myself." She hesitated, her eyes sweeping over his face. "Is there anyone at all you are suspicious of? I can investigate."

He took quick strides to stand by her side again. "Patience, please. Let me take care of this alone. I can't be worrying over your safety while I'm away." He looked into her eyes, willing her look of resolve away. She could be a stubborn woman.

She sighed, and he saw defeat in her eyes. He smiled and couldn't help pulling her to him one last time. He kissed her softly, never wanting to stop. But he did.

"I suppose I can take this time to discover why Mama is so against your family," her eyes cleared, her smile returning.

His jaw clenched at the mention of her mother. "Yes," he said. "Do that."

The cold, hard truth entered his mind. Daniel had nearly thrown away the security of his family for love.

Walter knew now that no matter if Patience learned the reason to her mother's aversion to him, that he could not marry her without the blessing of her parents. The cost to keeping his family secure meant he had to sacrifice love for duty.

He would need to find a wealthy woman whose

parents did not have such an aversion to him. With his growing status in London, he was sure he could make connections. He now had an estate to bolster his value. Why was he still unacceptable in Patience's parents' eyes?

Walter felt sick to his stomach. His eyes locked on Patience—her fair, smooth skin, her auburn curls, the dimple near her mouth. He couldn't have her. It was final.

"You must go now," he said, moving to unlock the door.

Patience hesitated, sensing his mood had shifted. She was sensitive that way. Another thing he loved about her.

"Have I done something wrong?" she asked quietly.

He shook his head. "No." The word came out breathy, strained.

She clasped her hands in front of her. "Then I'll see you when you return?"

"Undoubtedly." It wasn't necessarily a lie. It was likely they would cross paths again. He could no longer entertain the thought they could be together.

Patience slowly walked to the door. Turning to face him before leaving, she placed her hand on his arm. Her touch put all his senses on edge, nearly undoing his resolve.

"Be careful," she whispered.

He wanted to scoop her into his arms, hold her tight,

breathe in her rose scent one last time. But he knew how that would shake his resolve.

"You too," he answered instead.

He walked her to the front door and let her go, watching as she left. She turned to look back, smiling. He blew her a kiss as his heart shattered. It could very well be their last farewell. And she didn't even know it.

CHAPTER 10

LINCOLN'S INN greeted him like a second home, the familiar scents welcoming him into the grand old building. Walter walked straight to Mr. Welch's office to discuss the Vanderbilt case.

When he entered the old barrister's office, Mr. Welch's wrinkled gray eyes widened in surprise.

"Mr. Longman! I didn't expect you so soon."

"Only for a day or two," he said quickly. "I wanted to reaffirm my dedication to the Vanderbilt case. I have received your letters and reviewed every detail, memorizing them. I've already hashed out a strategy. But some things aren't adding up. I need to do some investigation to make sure I'm going down the right path."

He didn't know when he would be able to make

time to devote to both cases. He needed to find who murdered Daniel and why, but his ability to provide for his family hinged on solving the Vanderbilt case.

Mr. Welch held up a hand, and Walter slowed his speech to a stop. His mentor cocked his head in confusion. "You are returning to Wallingford?"

"Yes, just for another few days." Walter watched anxiously as Mr. Welch steepled his fingers together.

"My dear boy, I understand how much this case means to you."

"Everything, sir." He broke in, his mouth going dry. He sensed Mr. Welch's next words would not be pleasant.

"The council—myself included—believe you are under too much stress and trauma at this time. They wanted to go ahead and reassign the case to Mr. Bamber, but I convinced them to hold off a few more days. Time is not on your side, Mr. Longman."

Walter leaned over Mr. Welch's desk. His hands splayed over the cool wood. "I swear to you I can handle this case." His voice was earnest. "I only have a few more matters to wrap up at home, then I'll be here, devoid of distractions."

He pushed the picture of Patience to the back of his mind. He'd already decided about her. All he needed to do was put his plans into action and pray it didn't take her too long to get over him. He knew it might never happen for him.

Mr. Welch peered up at Walter, his lips pressed firmly together. Walter held his breath, waiting for the answer he sought. Finally, his mentor let out a long sigh, leaning back in his chair.

"I trust you, Mr. Longman. I will keep the council at bay for a few days more. But this case can't wait forever, and it needs England's sharpest minds devoted to it."

"I understand, sir." Relief rushed through Walter, pierced by some slight anxiety. Small doubts pressed on him as he wondered if he truly was the best person for the case. With everything he was currently dealing with, he was already worn too thin for his liking.

"Thank you," Walter said. "I won't disappoint." He hoped he would be able to make good on his promise.

"See that you don't," Mr. Welch said. "Your reputation isn't the only one on the line here. I have vouched for you, knowing you have the capacity to rise to the top. Do not let me regret my choice."

Walter gave him a curt nod before leaving the room. On his way out of the building, he passed Mr. Bamber's office. Unfortunately, his door was open.

Walter heard the hurried scrape of a chair and the quick steps as Mr. Bamber caught up to him. "Back again?" he asked, falling into step at Walter's side. "It's about time. We were starting to wonder if you'd fallen off the face of the earth."

Walter clenched his jaw, not slowing his walk. "I haven't, as you can clearly see," he said. "I'm not giving up the case, Bamber."

"I imagine you're not." Mr. Bamber gripped Walter's shoulder, forcing him to stop. He stiffened at the unwanted contact, staring into Bamber's long face. "Don't fool yourself. You are the least suitable person to take on this case, what with the family trauma you're going through. If Vanderbilt is not found guilty, that's on you."

Walter shook Mr. Bamber off him, knowing full well that the man was just trying to scare him off the case. "I am very capable of handling the case, thank you. Now if you'll excuse me—"

He turned on his heel, his coat ruffling past in his haste to get away from the man, and exited the building, feeling the heat build until he felt the thrum of his heartbeat in his head.

He would not let Mr. Bamber get inside his mind. He would win the case and build credibility and status. He would save his family from their debts by pursuing a wealthy woman whose money would dig them out of the hole they were stuck in. The thought turned his insides. It was easily said, but the practice would be another thing entirely. He pushed those thoughts from his mind and took a hackney to the theater district. It was time to confront Miss Gabriella Fox.

The Haymarket Theatre looked dark and uninhabited, with tall white pillars resolutely guarding the entrance. Taking a deep breath, he plunged between them, opening the front doors and stepping inside. The Theater's musty smell mixed with wax and cigar smoke. The scent turned his mind to the candle wax factory from his village, and a dark feeling entered the pit of his stomach.

Not a soul could be seen at the front, so Walter pressed on, walking deeper into the theater. He thought he heard voices shouting and opened a wide door, exposing a long line of red velvet seats leading up to a stage.

Walter took in the scene. The theater was nicer than he had imagined for being in the shady part of town where both wealthy gentlemen and poor came to be entertained. He highly doubted women of status were ever found here. Which only deepened the mystery.

Four people stood on the stage, three men and one woman, dressed in Roman attire, reciting lines. The woman's sheer dress plunged far below her neckline, revealing more cleavage than was proper. He averted his gaze, sick that his brother would associate himself with the place. Another man stood at the foot of the stage, watching. He suddenly waved his hands, shouting.

"No! Brutus, you are miserable. Absolutely miserable. Do you want a tomato in your face? Put more *feeling* into your words."

The man—Brutus—scowled in obvious disgust but didn't argue. The woman looked at both of them in irritation, then lounged across a loveseat, plucking at the armrest.

Walter took this moment to make himself known. He stepped forward, walking between the rows, all the actors' eyes turned to him.

Their director, noticing their gazes, turned, his dark mustache bristling. "Do you *mind,* sir? We are in the middle of a rehearsal."

"Apologies. I must speak to a Gabriella Fox. It is of the utmost importance."

The actress rose from the loveseat. "I am she." She looked down at him under heavily painted eyelids, her now curious eyes taking in all of him.

"A pleasure," he said through tight lips. "May I have a word in private?"

"You cannot speak with her now," the director whirled on him. "You will have to wait until after the rehearsal is finished."

Miss Fox held her hand out to stop the director's ravings.

"Marcus, stop your shouting." She turned her eyes back to Walter. "You may wait in my dressing room." She pointed toward a side exit. "It's the third door to the right. I'll be in shortly."

"Thank you," Walter nodded.

He left the actors to their work, following Miss Fox's instructions. He found her room, hesitating outside the closed door. It was improper for him to wait about in a lady's room, but he needed answers. He opened the door and stepped inside, taking in the lavish decorations.

The cloying scent of perfume assaulted his senses. Racks of dresses and capes lined one end of the room, a mirror on the other. An assortment of toiletries littered the vanity. Lavish furniture sprawled through the small dressing room, crowding it.

Coughing from the fumes, Walter sat on a piece of the uncluttered furniture and waited.

Within ten minutes, the door opened, and Miss Fox floated into the room, her dress trailing behind her. Walter quickly stood, uncomfortable with the whole situation.

"Forgive me for the wait," she said, taking a seat at her vanity and unclasping large earrings. "What did you say your name was?"

Walter winced at the informality. "My name is

Walter Longman. I believe you knew my brother, Daniel."

Miss Fox froze, slowly lowering her hands, setting the second earring in a jewelry box. "Yes, I believe we've met."

Walter clenched his jaw at her secretive voice. "I believe you and my brother were having a romantic affair."

Miss Fox laughed. "Mr. Longman, I would hardly describe your brother as romantic." She turned in her seat to face him, her indiscreet gown showing too much of her womanly features. Walter averted his eyes as she continued. "He visited the theater a time or two, presented me with flowers, and said he'd like to *court* me. Penniless as I am, he was like a prince." Her eyes narrowed. "But it quickly became clear, those were mere words. He had no real intention of making me *comfortable*." She looked back to her mirror.

Walter frowned. "Are you aware that he's recently passed away?"

She pressed her red lips together. "I was not."

Frustration blossomed in Walter. "His death may have resulted in foul play. Would you know of anyone who might have wished harm on Daniel?"

She laughed again, a high staccato trill. "Dear me, I hardly knew the man."

"Are there any details you could provide me about your interactions?" Walter pressed.

"I should not say. Our interactions were private and not for me to disclose."

Walter blanched. "Did you—" he stopped, unable to fathom the idea that Daniel would throw his future away for one such as she.

Her brows raised, looking at him under hooded eyes. "What, sir? You cannot be oblivious of nature," she stated dryly.

Walter's temper flared. The whole situation was beneath him. "Did he pay you for... unsavory services?"

Her grin stretched, and Walter sickened at her lack of remorse for Daniel's death. "Not everyone finds them unsavory," she purred. Then she sobered, her smile disappearing. "No. I'm an actress, not a prostitute. I don't take money for... *unsavory* favors."

She was trying to put an air of respectability about her, but he was not fooled.

"Then why meet privately?" he pushed.

Miss Fox traced her finger along the edge of her jewelry box. "We talked," she said slowly. "About life. Family. He was caring, something you don't often find. Too softhearted for my liking. I really think he was smitten with me though." She cast Walter an unpleasant look. "But he knew his family wouldn't approve. I suppose I don't blame you lot." She stood, her gown rustling. "Are we finished?"

Walter grappled for more questions. He hadn't gained any information to bring him closer to finding Daniel's murderer.

"Do you care at all?" he finally blurted. "That he's dead?"

Her dark brows lifted. "Of course, I do," she said, though nothing in her tone suggested so. "I'm sorry for your loss. Such a tragic accident." She gestured to the door. "The exit is on your left."

Walter turned to leave, his mind spinning, then froze with his hand on the doorknob, slowly turning back.

"Accident?" he repeated. "I never told you how he died."

For a moment, a look of vulnerability crossed her face, before she quickly recovered. "I assumed he was in some sort of accident. He was a healthy man."

Walter's eyes narrowed.

Irritation replaced her worry. "I believe you've overstayed your welcome, Mr. Longman. If you do not leave, I will have you escorted out."

Walter left the dressing room. Everything about this encounter was not right, and he would get to the bottom of it at all cost.

Even though coming here went against his every natural instinct, their hunch had been right. Miss Fox most definitely had something to do with Daniel's death. The only question was why. If he could get to the bottom of that answer, he felt he would know everything.

He pulled in a deep breath of air that wasn't clotted with perfume and moved down the small hall, ready to be as far away from this place as was humanly possible. He would return this evening. There was more here to discover.

CHAPTER 11

THE MURMUR of the crowd waiting outside the theater buzzed in Walter's ears. He stood in line at the ticket booth, holding a bunch of flowers as a distraction to blend in. His pulse quickened as he prepared to play his part. The evening was vitally important, though he'd need to get through tonight's performance. He hoped the information he gleaned would fill in the holes in Miss Fox's story. His instinct had to be correct. He had nothing else to go on, and his attention needed to get back to his case in London.

Walter shook his head, watching as well-dressed gentlemen and the working class filtered into the theater, loud and abrasive. How did his brother come to love Miss Fox? Was he truly taken by her beauty, or was there something more to his attraction?

It wasn't completely out of the question that Daniel

would have attended such an establishment for pleasure. Many of his station had. Daniel carried a lot of pressure on his shoulders. He wished to understand his brother's motivations, but found he couldn't.

Cavorting with an actress… that seemed largely out of character and highly irresponsible.

Walter purchased his ticket and entered the theater, mingling with the crowd. Spirits were being consumed, and Walter couldn't imagine how this crowd would be by the end of the night. He found his seat, settling himself into the red velvet chair near the back rows. Waiting for the performance to begin as raucous laughter echoed around him, his thoughts wandering to Patience.

What would she think of his being here, attending a performance? He determined to shelter her from the knowledge. She had already been through too much with her escapades in London. His eyes clouded over as he realized he had no right to be her protector, though everything in him longed for it to be different.

The performance began and Walter felt heat rise to his cheeks. He finally averted his eyes as the inappropriateness of the show sank in. He tried to cool his anger at Daniel and his affection for such raucous entertainment.

He brought his attention back as Miss Fox entered

the stage, dressed in a low-cut gown. Walter shook his head, amazed at his brother's attraction to her.

Some of her words didn't sound right to him. She had been careless, as if Daniel had only been an escape to a better life and nothing more. But he'd read over her letters. It had dripped with longing, imploring Daniel to see her again. Either she had been lying about their relationship... or she'd been lying to Daniel.

Walter took one look at the curved smile on her lips and drew his own conclusions: she had been acting. Whatever love Daniel thought she had for him was just for show. Likely the moment she realized he couldn't marry her, she ceased caring for him.

He couldn't bear to watch any longer. Standing, he pushed his way past drunken men and found himself in the foyer where more gentlemen gathered, smoking and laughing.

He wondered, had Patience come any closer to discovering why her mother was so opposed to him? He instantly berated himself. It wouldn't matter if she did. He wouldn't be asking for her parents' blessing a second time. His family came first, and the best way to take care of his family was to marry a wealthy woman.

He hated the idea of finding a partner he would not be attracted to. Even the thought of falling in love with another woman was abhorrent to him. No matter who he ended up marrying, he would always love Patience. *I should let her know that.*

Applause sounded from inside the theater, bringing him out of his musings. The doors opened, and swaying men spilled out. Their ruckus deepened the more crowded the lobby became.

Walter clutched the wilting flowers to his side and made his way down the corridor leading to the dressing rooms. He knew he would not be lucky enough to get another audience with Miss Fox, but if he could observe her and get a feel for the company that surrounded her, he knew he would find at least something to piece together.

He found the dressing rooms and pressed himself against the wall as patrons and actors alike poured from the theater hall. Walter spotted the black ringlets of Miss Fox while nudging closer, keeping out of sight. She was laughing with whom he could only assume were her admirers—well-dressed gentlemen loomed over her like she was a possession, their eyes straying unabashedly from her face.

One man caught his attention, and Walter stilled, his eyes widening. He recognized the protruding belly, flabby face, and small black eyes of Silas Pincock, the Baron of Danbury. Lord Danbury often frequented the House of Commons, where he'd seen him with Mr. Bamber. The two made a perfect pair.

He hadn't liked the man. Lord Danbury was loud and eccentric, but it surprised Walter to see him here. He kept back as he watched Lord Danbury dip his head, talking directly into Miss Fox's ear. She winced away, then nodded her head toward her dressing room. The two of them disappeared inside alone. Walter's heart rate increased as he suspected this was not a coincidence with too many connections—to him. His heart sank. Could the baron have something to do with Daniel? What could this mean?

A man next to the pair groaned, outwardly displaying his displeasure that only Lord Danbury enjoyed the company of Miss Fox this evening.

Another man scoffed, "They say money can't buy happiness… I would be happy to have an hour alone with Miss Fox any day!"

Walter scowled.

Eventually, the crowd cleared as it became clear Miss Fox would not be emerging from her dressing room soon.

Alone, his stomach churning, Walter approached the dressing room door, leaning his ear against the wall, hoping to catch something—anything—that would give him a hint as to what Lord Danbury and Miss Fox were discussing.

The hall still echoed with loud laughter, and he found it difficult to hear anything. He knew Lord

Danbury couldn't stay quiet for long. The longer one conversed with him, the louder his voice became.

Walter stood beside the door, his mangled flowers still clutched in his hand. He strained to listen, filtering out the background noise. He was rewarded when Lord Danbury's voice increased.

"His *brother,* eh?"

Walter strained to hear more. He caught a word. It could have been carriage. It could have been marriage.

"What's this here then?" an annoyed voice said from beside Walter.

Walter startled, turning to face a man smoking a cigar, his coat tails covered in flecks of ash.

"Waiting for a chance with the miss?"

Walter shook his head. "No, no."

The man's eyes fell to the flowers.

Walter cleared his throat. "I was sent... by my brother. To give these to her, but she seems otherwise engaged."

"I'll say," the man said, blowing smoke into Walter's face. "Lord Pinprick or what's his name is always meddling around here. You'd think he'd give another bloke a chance."

Walter raised his brows. "Excuse me?"

The man shook his head, sighing. "Forget it. Did you enjoy the show tonight?"

Walter hesitated. "It... wasn't my cup of tea."

The man laughed, loud and obnoxious. "You don't say? Them gals got ya blushing, then?"

Walter needed to leave.

Lord Danbury's voice grew louder, and the man who'd interrupted inched toward the door.

"Not a word, Miss Fox. It's our little secret."

Walter moved past the smoking man. "Excuse me," he mumbled, moving away before the couple emerged.

He moved down the dingy hall, dropping the limp flowers in the bin before stepping through an exit. The cool night air welcome against his face. The actress and baron knew each other.

CHAPTER 12

BACK IN HIS FLAT, Walter paced the room, mulling over Miss Fox and her connection to Lord Danbury. Walter still only had a suspicion. The things he overheard were only snippets, and though he could connect the pieces, he needed solid evidence and questions answered. It made no sense. Could Lord Danbury be involved in Daniel's death? The man was a peer.

He never liked the Baron. For similar reasons, he didn't care for Mr. Bamber. They were both snide and thought only to further their own ambitions and were contemptuous of anyone beneath them.

Walter sat on his bed, planting his face in his hands. Had he known his brother had fallen so far, he would have dropped everything to help him. He would have gone over the finances with Daniel, actively searched for a suitable wife, gotten him away from the brashness of the company he'd kept.

Walter's thoughts wandered back to Mr. Bamber. His fists tightened in frustration. The man was in a pinch with the council because he had botched up a handful of cases over the past year. He likely wanted the Vanderbilt case to re-establish his credibility. But did he have other reasons? Walter thought about Mr. Bamber. He didn't know much about the man or his background. He didn't even know if Mr. Bamber had a wife or children.

He stood, forming a plan. He would go to the Court House tomorrow and see how deeply Lord Danbury was entrenched in the political atmosphere. Walter didn't know if there was a connection, but something in the report of the Vanderbilt case caused his senses to ping. He needed information as to Mr. Bamber and his connections. Perhaps he could glean additional information about the association with Lord Danbury.

He had planned to leave for Wallingford that evening.

Satisfied, he undressed, his mind reverting to Patience. He lingered on the image of her face, not having the heart to wish it away. Not after everything he'd witnessed tonight. He needed some comfort.

Mr. Welch swiped at his face, letting out a breath as he stared down at his notes. "Mr. Vanderbilt was arrested after a gentleman of importance staying at his inn was found murdered. Stabbed to death. Do you remember what led to the arrest?"

Walter straightened in his chair, reviewing the details he had studied since taking the case. "There was blood on his clothing, tucked under his bed."

"Good man. And what have you found out about Mr. Vanderbilt's defense?"

Walter cleared his throat. "Mr. Vanderbilt had an alibi. He was checking out two guests at the time of the murder. There is no clear motive. It appears the poor devil may have been framed."

Mr. Welch nodded. "After looking into the victim's history, we've discovered he had a problem with opium. He may have been killed after cheating his suppliers out of their money."

"Right. He often frequented the Blue Lotus."

"And the men there are known to be rough." Mr. Welch sat back in his seat, nodding. "I think you have something here, Mr. Longman. Mr. Vanderbilt will be out of prison as soon as we prove his innocence. But we need to find out who killed the heir presumptive, Viscount of Highfield. The crown wants this solved, and they will not let this go without solid proof of guilt placed elsewhere." His gaze locked on Walter. "The trial is scheduled this time next week."

Walter nodded. His heart felt like it shot up into his throat. "Yes, sir. I'll be here." This didn't give him enough time in Wallingford to find answers to some questions nagging him about Daniel's murder. But he was grateful his mentor listened to his suspicions. Walter knew other men would not have been as confident in his abilities.

Mr. Welch nodded in satisfaction.

Walter hesitated, then leaned forward, lowering his voice. "What can you tell me about Mr. Bamber?"

Mr. Welch snorted, fishing for his pipe. "What do you want to know?"

"Who is he acquainted with?"

"An odd question, Mr. Longman." Mr. Welch leaned back, struck a flint before lighting his pipe, holding it between his teeth. "He's commonly found among the elite, I believe. They like to have talented lawyers in their pockets." He winked.

Walter frowned. "And why would that be?"

Mr. Welch shrugged. "When you're wealthy, things can get out of hand, and before you know it, a law's been broken and their reputation is on the line."

"Is Lord Danbury the type to break the law?" Walter asked.

Mr. Welch laughed. "The Baron? No, I don't believe

so. The poor man can be eccentric, but who can blame him? He's lost three wives in his lifetime. That could make any man a bit odd."

Walter jolted at this additional information. "Three wives, that seems excessive. What happened to them?"

"I don't know the details. I just know the jokes floating around town." The head barrister smiled. "Word is he's looking for a fourth wife. Only thing is, all the ladies think he's jinxed with bad luck. The mommas don't want their daughters to be the next unlucky wife, no matter how much blunt he has."

Mr. Welch laughed, and Walter forced a smile, but his head was spinning, absorbing all the information. "Who else does Mr. Bamber spend his time with?"

Mr. Welch narrowed his eyes. "Why such an interest in the man?"

"He seems to be vying for my position on our current case," Walter said. "I just want to know who I'm up against."

Mr. Welch puffed on his pipe for a moment, his face growing sober. He looked to the closed office door, then at Walter. Removing the pipe from his mouth, he leaned forward, lowering his voice.

"I shouldn't be telling you this…. But you have the right to know."

Walter's ears pricked at the secrecy in Mr. Welch's voice as his hands clenched in his lap.

"Mr. Bamber has been presenting the council with arguments of his own about the Vanderbilt case. He's not being paid, but he's looking more and more appealing. It's a good thing you'll be back for the first trial, because if you weren't, the position would have gone to him."

Walter's brows knit together. "Why does he want this case so badly?"

"Well…" Mr. Welch's voice dipped lower. "He's been on the wrong side of one too many cases, as you know. But more than that… if he had won this case, he would have been promoted as head barrister."

Walter cocked his head. "But you're head barrister in this council."

Mr. Welch licked his lips. "I'm retiring after this case."

Walter's eyes widened. "I didn't know."

"I haven't told many people. I'm not sure how Mr. Bamber found out. But he's next in seniority, so it makes sense he'd replace me. He's just had so many mess-ups that the council is open to promoting someone else." He shrugged. "Perhaps it will be you as head barrister, depending on your upcoming performance. You've proven to be effective in your occupation thus far."

Things began to fall into place. Of course Mr. Bamber was upset that Walter had gotten the case. If Mr.

Bamber didn't get the promotion, it wasn't likely he would get it for another several years, if ever. He would be stuck where he was until he retired, making half what he could be making as head barrister.

But if Walter made head barrister—a rush of adrenaline hit him at the prospect. He could easily pay off his debts. He could ask Patience to be his wife.

Hope blossomed in Walter until it turned into a flame. Now, more than ever, he had to win this case.

"I must leave you now, sir." His voice wavered as he stood. "I've got a few things to sort before returning to Wallingford."

"Very good, son. We'll get cracking on that case when you return."

Walter left the office and nearly ran outside. He turned toward the library, determined to find more information on Lord Danbury and his wives.

Rounding a corner, he almost rammed into the man himself.

Lord Danbury blinked, assessing Walter.

"Mr. Longman?" he sputtered. "May I offer my deepest condolences? I saw the tragedy in the paper, and Mr. Bamber was so kind as to provide me with the details."

Walter kept his features expressionless.

"Thank you," he said, stepping aside, moving past Lord Danbury.

"I'm surprised you've returned to London so soon." The baron's voice rose, causing Walter to halt. "I expect you are still grieving."

Walter turned, facing the gentleman. "Yes, I am. I'm well despite my family's loss, thank you. I have an important case that necessitated my return."

Lord Danbury's small eyes narrowed. "Ah, yes. Mr. Bamber has told me about it." The large man approached Walter, setting a heavy hand on his shoulder. He leaned in. His voice low. "Mr. Bamber has friends in high places." He breathed a puff of tobacco-filled air in Walter's face. "They would all like to see him take on this case. They'd like to see someone… more qualified. Someone who isn't distracted with grief."

Walter held Lord Danbury's eyes. He could not misunderstand the menacing tinge in his expression. He opened his mouth to confirm before the baron continued.

"If I were you, I'd return home and take care of that sweet mother and sister of yours," he paused. "Oh, yes, and Miss Hawthorn is your neighbor, correct? A lovely girl. I'd hate for any kind of harm to come to her."

Walter's blood chilled at the implication. Backing away, he bowed. "Good day, Lord Danbury."

The gentleman dipped his hat and proceeded on his way.

Walter picked up his pace as he hurried to the library. He had just been threatened. The baron had his reasons for wanting him off the case. An innocent man didn't threaten. His gut told him Lord Danbury was involved with his brother's murder or knew something about it. He entered the library and checked in with the attendant.

Moving to the vault, he pulled out all the pertinent records he could find on Lord Danbury. Setting at a table, he took notes as he poured over newspapers, gleaning any information he could find.

The death of his third wife was two years ago. The late Lady Danbury had grown suddenly ill and passed away from an unknown sickness.

Walter frowned, looking over the news from the weeks leading up to and following her death. He found an article claiming Lord Danbury had inherited the rest of her assets after her passing, increasing his fortune considerably.

Walter continued reading as a shudder ran through his body. Each one of Lord Danbury's wives had died from some unknown illness, all with the same symptoms. All but the first Lady Danbury. She had fallen from a cliff into the sea while they were away on holiday.

Walter's fingers grew icy. Everyone knew Lord

Danbury was eccentric and a bit of a lady's man, but no one could ever suspect…

He stared at the drawings of each wife—young, from wealthy families. His stomach lurched as his suspicions rose. Lord Danbury could have killed each of his wives to increase his fortune. It seemed unlikely they would have all died so young. Two of illness and one by an accident. If it was truly an accident. If Lord Danbury wasn't afraid to take a life, even that of a lifelong companion, what else was he capable of?

A lovely girl, Lord Danbury's words hit him like a battering ram. *I'd hate for any kind of harm to come to her.*

Patience.

Walter put the papers back into the archive and hurried from the library. His only thoughts were of Patience and her safety.

CHAPTER 13

P ATIENCE COULDN'T SIT IDLY by, doing nothing, while Walter was in London. Had he any new clues as to the carriage accident? The waiting was torture. She wished to help solve the murder. She determined to investigate the new groom and maid's past, if only to give her something useful to do while she awaited Walter's return. She and Henrietta used to be friends. It was time she made a call and offer her condolences. She hadn't been to the estate since her parents refused Walter.

Henrietta wouldn't mind the company. She could ask about the maid and the groom that Daniel hired. Henrietta would know more than Walter, since she had been home at the time of their employment.

In the guise of riding, she changed into her riding habit, and pinned her hat to her head. She slipped down the back stairs, avoiding her mother as she made her way to the stables. A stable hand had her mare ready within the hour, and she soon had her horse galloping across the field.

She loved this time of year. The summer had cooled into fall and the air had that crisp feel, like winter was just around the corner.

Making her way to the front of the manor, a groom took her mare as she walked to the door. Patience banged the large brass knocker at the entrance, then stepped back and waited.

The butler opened the door. "How may I assist you, miss?"

She smiled at the old man who had been serving the Longman family for as long as she could remember. "I'm here to visit Miss Henrietta. Is she accepting callers?"

"Right this way, miss," he sniffed, stepping aside, letting her into the front parlor.

"Thank you." She settled on a chair while she waited for Henrietta.

Her eyes wandered to the paintings hanging on the walls, then to the vases of wilted funeral flowers lined up along the mantel.

Footsteps sounded from the hallway, then Henrietta entered, looking at Patience in surprise.

"Miss Hawthorn. I wasn't expecting your visit today."

Patience stood. "I was hoping to give you some company, Henrietta. We haven't talked in so long." She hoped she wasn't intruding on the girl. She had been closer to Walter's age and had always gravitated toward him instead of his sister.

Henrietta looked at Patience, her eyes still sad about losing her brother.

"I haven't seen many people since the accident."

Patience's heart fell. This entire time she had been giving all her worries to Walter, forgetting that his family had been grieving as well, if not more so because they had depended on Daniel for so much.

"I understand, and I'm sorry I've stayed away for so long. I should have remembered you and not just Walter."

Henrietta looked to her with questioning eyes, and rightfully so. After things fell apart with her brother and then being brought back from London so suddenly, it was a wonder anyone in the neighborhood welcomed her at all.

Henrietta paused, glancing awkwardly at her, and Patience took this as her opportunity. She looked around, trying to communicate her true purpose in coming.

"It's especially tidy in here. Did you acquire a new maid?"

Henrietta looked around, a frown creasing her brow. She looked like Walter when she frowned.

"Yes, I believe so. Anna. She's a sweet woman. About your age." Henrietta gestured to the loveseat. "Please, won't you sit down?"

Patience complied. "How are you faring? Is there anything I can do to help ease your burdens?"

Henrietta sat gracefully across from Patience and clasped her hands in her lap.

"I'm as well as one might expect. I suppose only time will dull the pain, but it will never go away. Not completely." She lifted her eyes to Patience. "I've been writing a new song to pass the time. Would you like to hear?"

"Yes, I certainly would," Patience said, thankful to have more time in Walter's home.

Henrietta led her to another room where the pianoforte stood against bay windows. "Do you play? I can't remember."

"Not well," Patience admitted.

Henrietta sat at the pianoforte and began a melancholy song, infused with whatever grief she carried. Patience felt for Walter's young sister and wondered if there was more to offer the girl in support, for Patience knew what it was like to have little hope of the future to anchor one's feelings to.

Henrietta played another melancholy song, and

Patience soon became weary of the depressing tunes of the minor chords. She stood as Henrietta finished.

"I am thirsty. Do you think it is almost time for tea?"

"Oh, I am sorry. Yes, let me fetch Mama."

Henrietta stood, but Patience waved her down.

"No, it would be a delight if you would continue playing. You have such a wonderful talent. I can find a maid."

Henrietta hesitated, then took her seat again behind the pianoforte and began playing yet another dreary song.

Patience took a relieved breath before ducking out of the room. She walked up the stairs to the study. She wanted to search for any more useful records Daniel had kept regarding the new hires. Walter had been so focused on that letter she was sure there was something they missed. The house was quiet, and she didn't encounter any servants. Opening the door softly, she quietly entered the study, closing the door behind her. Going to the cupboards first, looking through the nooks and crannies. She knew she shouldn't be snooping, but Walter had practically given her permission. She kept an ear out for the music downstairs, its melancholy tones easily sounding through the house.

She found the book she sought with information of the servants. She scanned the new groom's documentation. He'd come with good references from respectable people in the neighborhood, names she recognized. There didn't seem to be anything suspicious, though it didn't seem they needed another groom. Why would Daniel have overstaffed the house? Perhaps Daniel had been planning on purchasing more horses.

Setting aside the groom's documentation, she found the maid's. Anna Hopkins seemed to have gone from household to household, hardly able to keep a job, though there was no mention of Anna's shortcomings in the file.

Patience frowned, scanning the list of her previous employers. Her heart nearly skipped a beat as she read the well-known name. Lord Danbury. Anna had worked in his household for two years, being dismissed after Lord Danbury's latest wife had passed away.

Patience listened when she noticed silence echoed throughout the house. Henrietta had stopped playing. She quickly gathered up the documents and stuffed them back into the file, replacing them into the drawer. When the keys of the pianoforte began tinkling again, Patience relaxed. She needed to return to Henrietta before they caught her snooping.

Patience stepped back into the corridor when a movement caught the corner of her eye. Patience looked up at a maid with light brown hair pulled back into a bun, staring, her eyes narrowed.

"What's all this, miss?" the maid asked.

Patience wavered, trying to think up an excuse. "Henrietta asked if I might fetch her a shawl. I believe I got lost."

It was clear the maid didn't believe her.

"I reckon I'd best ask Henrietta about that shawl," she said slowly.

Patience bit her lip. "Are you Anna?"

The maid's frown deepened. "Who wants to know?"

"My name is Patience. Patience Hawthorn. I have a few questions for you."

The maid looked taken aback for a moment, but she quickly replaced her scowl. "What questions?"

As the music still hung in the air, Patience took courage. "I wanted to know… where you were the day Daniel Longman died."

Anna's eyes lit, and Patience wasn't sure if she liked the way Anna's lips quivered into a little smirk. "I can show you if you like."

Surprised at the maid's answer, she nodded her head, accepting the offer. "By all means," she said.

Anna led her down the servant's stairs, wiping her hands on her apron. "Mr. Longman was a kind soul he was," she said over her shoulder as Patience followed. "Took me on when no one else would."

"Why ever not?" Patience inquired, relieved she was finally getting somewhere.

Anna opened the back door, leading Patience out into the back gardens.

"Too much history," Anna said darkly. "One master couldn't bear the sight of me and sent me off. Another didn't like the way I polished his shoes and sent me packing. One's child died in my arms—nothing I could do. The child was sickly—blamed me and let me go. It's been a hard life, miss."

This was true enough, but the maid's smirk set something off in Patience and she instantly put her guard up, watching the maid carefully as she led her through the gardens toward a thicket of trees just ahead. She was a woman of unfortunate circumstances but was it entirely coincidental? Anna had a child die in her care, Lord Danbury's wife had passed away while she was there, and now Daniel... It was too coincidental.

Patience stopped in her tracks when Anna made no sign of slowing.

Realizing Patience was no longer following, Anna turned to face her. "Coming, miss?"

"I... I don't want to leave Henrietta's company entirely. Not while she's expecting me back any moment."

"It's not far," Anna promised. "There's something there you should see."

Patience hesitated, looking at the thick trees and underbrush ahead. She and Walter used to play there. A small candle factory lay just off Walter's property, but not much else stood near it. Why would Anna be out here?

Anna shrugged. "Fine by me. Mr. Longman had told me to keep it a secret, so a secret it shall remain."

Patience bit her lip as Anna walked back to the house. "Wait."

Anna turned. Her eyebrows raised.

Patience let out a breath. "Just hurry, please."

Anna nodded. "Right this way, miss."

Patience followed her into the thicket, which turned into a dense forest. Squirrels and birds chattered in the trees, giving Patience comfort as she walked.

"How much farther?" she asked.

"Nearly there."

Patience's senses heightened, her heart beating in her eardrums as she realized they were indeed heading for the candle factory. The situation she was in made little sense. Why was a maid showing a complete stranger a potential secret of Daniel Longman's? Why would it be all the way out here in the first place?

The old factory cropped up in the underbrush. The caved-in roof was visible from afar. It was even more run down since she and Walter explored it when they were children. How long had it been? The years had slipped away.

Anna pointed. "In there."

Patience stopped, peering into the dark interior. Only patches of light filtered through the broken roof.

"We need not go any further," she said, doubtful of the maid's motives.

"It's safe," Anna assured, though it did not bring much comfort as Anna's hands twisted in the fabric of her dress.

Anna's eyes flickered from tree to tree as if she were nervous.

Patience felt unsettled, something in the maid's behavior. It was time to leave, return to the house. Henrietta would wonder where she'd gone. But something inside her urged her to continue on. If she were to find the answers to Daniel's murder, Walter would come back to her. Let her share his life, even without her parents' blessing. She was sure the maid knew something.

Swallowing her misgivings, she stepped forward.

Anna entered the factory first, ducking through the rotting door. Taking a deep breath, Patience moved inside behind her, confident she could stave off the maid if she were attacked.

A weird thought. Her imagination was running wild.

She stopped just inside, letting her eyes adjust to the darkness while she looked for Anna. Where had she gone? Her eyes focused, then her blood ran cold. A sinking feeling settled into her heart.

She'd walked into a trap.

Walter's face flashed in her mind as the end of a shovel whizzed toward her head, giving her little time to react. She turned, splitting pain blossomed at the side of her skull, then she fell to her knees. The world darkened around her as she fell to the ground, her hands scraping against twigs, dried leaves, pain, then blackness.

CHAPTER 14

WALTER RODE on horseback into Wallingford in his haste to return promptly, thinking of his family and Patience.

He was always thinking of Patience.

Lord Danbury's threat had shaken him, and he needed to know his family was safe. He made it back to Wallingford in record time, only stopping twice to rest his horse before riding out again. He rode up the cobbled drive, praying to find his mother and sister safe, painting and playing the pianoforte. If everything was sound, he would check on Patience. He needed to inform her of everything he had learned. With the two of them working together, he was sure they could come up with the evidence he needed to bring Lord Danbury to justice.

He dismounted, ran up the steps, and stepped into

the hall. An unusual quiet met his ears. The pianoforte was silent. Henrietta had been drumming on the thing incessantly since his first arrival. It was her way of dealing with the loss, so he couldn't deny her the distraction.

It felt like his heart was in his throat as he ascended the stairs. "Henrietta!" he called. "Henrietta, are you here?"

A door to the drawing room opened, and his mother appeared. "Walter, whatever is the matter? Why are you shouting?"

Walter rushed to his mother, catching her elbows.

"Mother, have you seen Henrietta?"

His mother blinked, alarm welling in her eyes. "Yes, she was at dinner not half an hour ago. Tell me what has happened, Walter."

He turned toward Henrietta's room, leaving his mother standing in the hall.

"Henrietta?" He knocked loudly on her closed door.

"Leave me alone." Her voice sounded thick with anguished sobs.

His concern spiked as he twisted the knob, pushing the door open to find Henrietta laying on her bed, hugging a pillow. Tears streaked down her face. She was otherwise unharmed, though she cast him an icy glare.

"I told you to leave me alone," she whimpered.

Walter slowly sat on the edge of her bed as his mother entered behind him, hovering in concern.

"Why are you crying, Henrietta?" he gently asked.

They had all been through so much as of late.

His sister buried her face in her pillow. "I don't want to talk of it," she mumbled through the cushion.

Walter looked to his mother, who had taken a seat on the opposite side of the bed. She bent to stroke her distraught daughter's hair. Henrietta turned to her mother as she softly comforted her daughter.

His mother looked up, concern in her eyes. "Miss Hawthorn came to see her this morning. Henrietta began playing for her, and Miss Hawthorn left without a word."

"She *hated* my music!" Henrietta wailed into her pillow.

Walter's heart twisted. This wasn't like Patience at all. "Miss Hawthorn was here? When did she leave?"

"Before noon, I imagine. That's when Henrietta realized her guest had left her while she was playing."

The story made little sense. "She just got up and... left? Without a word?"

"She left under the guise of getting the maid to ring for tea," Henrietta moaned, lifting her head. His mother nodded her confirmation.

Walter nearly cursed under his breath. He knew exactly what Patience had done. She'd gone to interrogate the servants, but why had she left without a word? The sickening answer penetrated his mind.

"Mother, have you noticed anything unusual from the servants?"

His mother frowned. "What an odd question to ask. Of course not."

Walter ground his teeth. "Where is the new maid? I want to speak with her."

"Anna?" His mother pursed her lips. "We haven't seen her all day. A shame, because she was supposed to finish the wash today. I must have a talk with her about how this house should be run. It is not the first time she has disappeared, neglecting her duties."

"You're saying she's missing?" Walter's mouth went dry.

His mother nodded. "Yes, I haven't seen her since noon."

About the time Patience went to ask for tea, he thought. "There is something I must attend to. Excuse me, Mother." He exited the room before anyone protested.

He needed to visit Patience to reassure himself everything was as it should be. Patience was safe, surely. At her mother's side, needlepoint in hand, wishing she was with him. He hoped it was just a coincidence that Anna and Patience had gone at the same time, but doubt niggled in his gut.

Walter went straight to the stable, retrieving his mount, who was still saddled. He untied the reins as Benjamin appeared. He noticed Patience's mount grazing in a stall. Strange, she wouldn't have left without her mare. Panic raised in his gut.

"Benjamin, I need you to gather the men and safeguard the house 'til I return. Do not let my mother and sister leave."

"Yes, sir." The groom's eyes widened.

He mounted, urging his horse forward, passing a carriage on his way down the road. He'd seen the carriage before, in London, but he had no time to stop. He must see that Patience was safe.

Patience winced, slowly peeling her eyes open, her head pounding in pain. The setting sun pierced through a broken window, blinding her. Groaning from the throb in her head, her hand moved to feel her temple, only to meet resistance. Her hands were fastened tightly behind her back. How long had she been lying here? Where was she? Memories muddled in her mind.

Anna. The factory.

She squinted, trying to look around, gauging her situation, but her head pounded, and her wrists burned from the rope. She closed her eyes, saying a silent prayer.

Leaves crunched across the ground. Patience opened her eyes, turning toward the sound. She could just make out Anna leaning against the stone wall.

Her heart sank.

A shovel stood within arm's reach of Anna, propped against the corner wall. Anna didn't smile as she watched Patience, her eyes glinting in the filtered light.

Patience licked her dry lips, appraising the situation, trying to remain calm.

"Let me go, Anna," she said slowly, trying to keep the fear from her voice. "I'll be missed. Do you want to lose your job?"

Anna shook her head. "My employer will arrive shortly."

"Your employer? What are you talking about? The Longman family employs you," Patience reminded the maid, her mind still spinning. "Please, just let me go."

Anna ignored her. Patience was about to implore again. She wasn't against groveling for her life, when the door rattled and opened. A bulky figure filled the frame, then stepped inside, coughing from the dust that swirled at his feet.

"My, this shabby place gets worse each time I visit."

Patience's eyes widened as they settled on Lord Danbury. He spotted her, visibly startled. "Miss

Hawthorn?" His eyes snapped to Anna. "Anna, what are you doing with this poor girl?"

"Lord Danbury, please release me!" Patience cried. "The maid is insane!"

"Miss Hawthorn. I'm baffled. Truly baffled." He lumbered over, lowering himself to the ground. He squatted beside her.

Patience twisted, lifting her tied wrists so he might undo them.

He took her wrists in his hands and fingered the ties. "Anna, why did you bring Miss Hawthorn here?"

"She was snooping, sir. Looking through the Longmans' things. Asking about me. About Mr. Longman's death. It's like she *knows.*"

Lord Danbury stilled, Patience's hands still in his. Her heart beat hard against her throat. "Lord Danbury, please…" He dropped her hands and she looked him in the eyes.

"Miss Hawthorn. Care to share any suspicions with me?"

"No!" Patience stuttered. "What is it I am to suspect?"

"Why are you looking into Daniel Longman's death?" Lord Danbury's charismatic smile had taken on a forced look.

"I'm not," she insisted.

He sighed, then looked to Anna.

Anna grasped the shovel.

For the first time, a nasty grin spread across her face. "Would you like me to take care of her, sir?"

Lord Danbury stood. "No, Anna. You've done enough already." He looked down at Patience as she squirmed, though it did her little good as her feet were tied as well.

"Well, this is a mess, isn't it?" He reached into his pocket and pulled out a small pistol, too petite in his meaty hands.

If she hadn't known the damage it could do, her fright might not have been complete.

"I'm afraid I'll have to dispose of you now," Lord Danbury mused. "And Walter, because that boy just doesn't know when to quit."

Patience's eyes widened as her breath came out in short, shallow gasps. "Why are you doing this?" she whispered.

Lord Danbury's lips pursed. "Alright, fine then. We can delay the inevitable." He stood, shifting from one foot to the other. "You don't think I've become wealthy from inheritance and petty investments, do you?" The glint in his gray eyes deepened. "I'm a dangerous man who doesn't like to follow the rules if I can help it."

Anna giggled from somewhere behind him, but Patience forced her concentration on the devil in front of her. He seemed to gloat in his evil as if he were proud.

"I need a barrister in my pocket. A greedy man who knows how to win. Mr. Bamber is one of the best and fits the bill. But your friend, or should I say lover?" His eyes scanned her body, chilling her to the bone. "Walter Longman has impeded Mr. Bamber's promotion. Anna here set up Vanderbilt by murdering an opium-addicted Peer and then placing damning evidence in Mr. Vanderbilt's rooms. It was a simple case to win, but one that also captured public interest. Two excellent things for my future plans."

Patience pieced together what Lord Danbury was saying. She didn't know much about Walter's case, the one he was working on to better his life, but never guessed there was a connection.

"You killed an innocent man," she rasped, "then framed another. All so Mr. Bamber could win and receive a promotion?"

"Precisely." Lord Danbury grinned as if pleased with himself. "I've played this game for years, Miss Hawthorn. I realized I could grow my fortunes faster with multiple wives." He shrugged. "So, I pushed my first wife off the cliff."

Patience's jaw dropped.

"The rest had more finesse—a bit of poison here, a bit of poison there. The doctors could never figure out what *illness* took my other two wives."

Her heart raced. Patience thought she might vomit. He wouldn't be confessing this if she were to live.

"I'm building my wealth bit by bit, Miss Hawthorn," he continued. "And I need Mr. Bamber as the head barrister to help me. When we learned Mr. Longman had a high possibility of being awarded the case, we quickly formed a plan. The death of his brother would be a sure way to get him out of London, and then Mr. Bamber would step in. It was all very clever until Longman poked around. He wouldn't give up. Wouldn't stay home. Become the country gentlemen when he had his chance."

Anger surged through Patience. "You killed Daniel just so you could get Walter off a case that *you* constructed?"

A sickening laugh bubbled from the Baron's throat. "Devious, isn't it? It's rather addicting, picking off souls one by one." He leveled his pistol at her. "I'm afraid you're next, Miss Hawthorn. Pity you got in my way. I thought you might be my next wife."

He looked to Anna. "Untie her. I like the thrill of the chase."

Patience held perfectly still, focusing on breathing while Anna cut her bonds loose. Everything in her screamed for her to run, but she knew it wouldn't make a difference. Lord Danbury would shoot her in the back.

She wasn't sure she *could* run, as petrified as she

was. Her ankles were sore. Her head ached, so she remained on the ground, cowering.

Anna kicked her in the ribs. "Get up," she demanded.

Shaking, Patience stood, stumbling over nothing. Bile rose to her throat as she faced Lord Danbury. He cocked the gun and slowly raised his arm, aiming as he advanced toward her.

"Not a runner, eh?" He was so close she could smell the tobacco on his breath. A thick finger ran from her cheekbone down to the base of her neck. She stiffened at his touch. "No matter. I prefer it this way. More intimate."

Patience had always thought of this old man to be an eccentric member of society. Too loud and clueless to be of any use to the world, but standing like this with his perfectly constructed plans, she knew it had just been an act. A clever illusion.

He pressed the pistol under her chin as she fought to hold tears back. She would not let him see her cry. Not give him the satisfaction he craved. She swallowed, gaining her composure.

Lord Danbury's free hand wandered down her waist to the outside of her thigh. She closed her eyes as he continued to fondle her. Refusing to remain silent any longer, a scream ripped from her throat. But Lord Danbury only laughed.

She heard a door crash amidst the commotion. Walter barged into the room, grappling with Lord Danbury, wrapping an arm around his neck. The pistol clattered to the floor, and with it Patience sank, trembling, her eyes wide as she watched Walter throw Lord Danbury against a wall, a fist beating into his ribs.

"You dog!" Walter seethed. "You *dare* lay a hand on her!"

Anna stepped back from the scuffle as her eyes frantically sought Patience, then focused on something next to her side. Patience followed her gaze to the pistol.

Anna leaped forward, and Patience crawled for the gun, refusing to let it enter the mad woman's hands. Her fingers curled around the pistol just as Anna barreled into her, knocking her back. Patience's head hit the stone wall, and for a moment it blinded her. Anna grasped the pistol, trying to wrench it out of her hand. Patience attempted to push her away, but she was strong for someone so small.

A shot rang through the building, and the room stilled. Patience froze, her breath taken away. She looked into Anna's eyes, which were lit with gleeful malice, then dimmed. Patience pulled away.

Blood covered her front. She looked back toward Anna. The light in her eyes lost focus, her smile pulled downward. She crumpled on top of Patience as they both fell to the floor. From somewhere in the room,

Patience heard Walter shout her name. Her ears ringing from the loud shot, her mind tried to grapple with what had just happened.

Strong hands pulled Patience from under Anna's body, and Walter's voice floated into her consciousness.

"Patience? Patience, heaven above, I thought she had shot you."

He was so close. So warm. She looked into his wide, desperate eyes and wrapped her arms around him, relieved. He pulled her closer, into a tight embrace. Sitting on the floor, they held each other. Anna's body lay beside them, her face turned away.

"Where is Lord Danbury?" Her eyes scanned the dim room, but he was nowhere in sight. Reality crashed in. He'd escaped.

Everything came crashing in, and she clutched Walter like a lifeline, a sob escaping her throat.

"It's alright," Walter soothed. "You're alright," he kissed her cheek. "You're safe. I'll never let you go, my love, never again." His grip tightened as she relaxed into him.

.

CHAPTER 15

PATIENCE PULLED AWAY FROM WALTER, her body still shaking as she looked around the room again. "Lord Danbury escaped?"

Walter grasped her arms, checking her over once more. "Yes. But he will not get far. I heard what he said. It's the evidence I needed. He will not be free long."

She nodded, letting the events of the day wash over her. Her head pounded harder. Wincing, she closed her eyes, willing herself to stay strong for Walter. She touched her head. A large bump was forming. She pulled her hand away. No blood, thank heavens.

Walter didn't need to worry about her condition among everything else. "How did you find me?" Her feet weakened beneath her.

Walter tightened his grip, sliding his arms around her waist, bringing her close to his chest.

"I passed Lord Danbury's carriage on the road to find you. It upset my sister when you left without saying your goodbyes. I almost rode on, but when I realized I'd seen the carriage before, I changed course and followed. I would have been here sooner if I hadn't lost him at the end." He trailed kisses down her cheek, but she pulled away.

"How did you know something connected Lord Danbury to this?"

He growled. "He threatened me in London. I figured it connected the case to Daniel's death. Why else would he threaten you and my family?" He shook his head as if clearing his mind.

"He threatened your family?"

He nodded. "I shouldn't have involved you, but I did. I did not understand it would put you in such danger. Patience, I would never hurt you intentionally."

Her head spun. She wasn't sure if it was because of Walter's sweet words or the knock on her head. "I know," she whispered, trying to calm his fears. "Can you take me home? I am feeling faint."

He looked concerned. "I will bring you to my home. It is closer, and my mother can call for the doctor while I fetch your parents."

"No! Please. Mama will not wish to set foot in your house, and I will have a hard time explaining this as it is. I do not wish her to know it has involved me with you. She demanded I stay away." She felt him stiffen and rushed on to explain. "Mama has never listened to my feelings concerning you. I do not wish to give her any more reasons for keeping us apart. If we return to my home together, I might not persuade her to accept our wishes." She hoped he saw the truth in her statement.

He relaxed and nodded, squeezing her one last time before releasing her. She tried to remain strong for him, but she instantly missed his arms and the support he'd given her.

"I—my horse is in your stables." Panic momentarily gripped her at the thought of returning home in her condition. Perhaps it was more sensible to return to Walter's house and call for a physician, but everything in her told her that would be an awful idea. She'd never had strength to go against her mother's wishes, and she was sure if she tested her mother now, she would lose all hope of having Walter in her life.

"I'll take you home on my horse, if you're not opposed to sharing the saddle with me," he hesitated. "I'll have my groom return your mare to your stables.

She nodded, "I think that is a splendid idea," flashing him a loving smile, giving in to his assistance, thankful for his presence. She would need it to face her mother in her condition after all.

He guided her out of the old building, holding her arm in support. She breathed in the fresh air. Thankful she was alive to experience this small blessing.

"What about Anna?"

"I'll send for the constable as soon as you're safe. I'm sure he'll have questions."

The feeling of euphoria disappeared the moment she stepped into the drawing room. Her mother's screams pierced Patience ears as her mother fussed about her.

Her eyes were wide, mouth gaping. "What happened?" Taking in Patience's disheveled state.

Patience looked down at the blood spattered over the front of her dress, and her heart sank. She forgot. She should have marched up to her room to change before confronting her parents.

"I'm alright, Mama," Patience said, but her mother had already spun on Walter, waving an accusing finger toward him.

Patience tried to get Walter to leave her on the steps, but he insisted they approach her parents together.

"You! You let her in harm's way. I demand an answer. Now!"

Her father stood near the fireplace, silent. He

reached out his arms, and Patience went to him, letting him enfold her in a rare embrace.

"Do not be angry at Walter," Patience said, turning, giving her mother a stern eye. "He did nothing wrong— he rescued me."

Her mother snorted. "You should have been nowhere near him. I ban the two of you from ever crossing paths again!"

Patience pulled herself from her father's embrace, stepping toward her mother. "I will not obey you," she seethed. "Walter is a good man. He saved my *life*—"

"Mrs. Hawthorn, if I may." Walter cleared his throat, clutching his riding gloves in both his hands. "I love your daughter more than life itself. My feelings of last summer have not changed. I beseech you—"

"No," her mother snapped. "No, I don't wish to hear any more from you, Mr. Longman. Depart at once."

"My financial and social status has changed," he continued, braving her mother's fury. "I have status in London and plan on settling in a small home with Patience at my side. There is no greater joy than I could imagine."

Her mother's face grew livid as she turned to her father. "Husband, force this man out. He is no longer permitted on our property."

Her father did not move as his eyes rolled from

Patience to Walter, then back to his wife. "I would like to hear Mr. Longman's offer," he said firmly.

Her mother's jaw dropped, and Patience ran to her father, embracing him again. "Thank you, Papa," she breathed.

Her mother leveled Walter with a stare. "Go on then," she nodded between gritted teeth.

Walter squeezed the riding gloves tighter. "I have regarded no one else in all my life with higher esteem than I do Patience. I dare come to you a second time for her hand because I believe our commitment to each other is worth the risk of a second rejection. I implore you to think of her happiness."

Her father nodded slowly, but her mother trembled in anger.

"I've heard enough of this. Patience, go to your room." She pointed her finger to the door, dismissing her like a child.

Patience broke at her mother's persistent refusal. She had endured enough of her mother's degradation. She held firm in her stance as she lifted her chin. "No, Mama. I love Walter. Would you really take that from me?"

"The answer is *no,* and that is final," her mother cried with a voice that bordered on hysteria. "It's for your own good, Patience. Mr. Longman, for the last time—leave us."

Patience met Walter's gaze. The warmth from his face ebbed away, replaced by frustration. Her heart broke when he turned on his heel and marched from the room.

The moment the door shut behind him, Patience whirled on her mother, tears blinding her. "Why are you doing this to me?" she demanded.

"Patience, one day you'll thank me," her mother's voice softening. "Trust me."

Patience wouldn't take no for an answer. "I will marry Walter," she growled. "I will marry him even without your blessing. I love him, and I don't care about his financial situation. You can't stop me from being happy."

Her mother grimaced as she looked at her daughter, then turned to her father. "Leave us for a moment, William."

He frowned at her mother. "Why?"

She grit her teeth. "Leave us!"

Patience felt sorry for her father. He had endured enough through the years. Any other gentleman would have put her in her place. Patience was sure of it. Grumbling, he marched through the door, slamming it closed behind him.

Her mother faced her, taking her hands in hers. "Patience, my dear. I've never told you, never wanted to burden you… but the Longman family deeply offended me long before you were born."

Patience's eyes widened, sure there were many people in her life that had offended her mother.

"What happened?" she whispered.

Her mother sighed. "I was young. Careless. Walter's father promised to marry me. I believed he loved me as ardently as I loved him."

Patience gaped at her mother. "Walter's father… he gave you an offer of marriage?"

Her mother nodded, pursing her lips together bitterly. "He backed out at the last minute. It broke my young heart. When I learned you had formed an attachment to Walter, I feared you would suffer the same heartache as I."

Patience shook her head. "That won't happen, Mama. Walter loves me." She paused. "And perhaps this union could put away past feuds and hurt feelings."

The door banged open, and her father came striding through.

"*This* is the reason you were against the Longman boy?" he demanded, his face twisted in hurt and anger, stunning both women into silence.

Her father leveled his wife with a stare. "You weren't just trying to protect our daughter. You wanted revenge. You wanted to crush that young man's heart to get back at his father." He shook his head. "Where is your head at, woman?"

He turned to Patience, taking her hand and raising it to his lips. "You have my blessing," he said gruffly. "Do with it as you will."

A shocked gasp escaped her throat. She had secured her father's blessing! She threw her arms around his neck. "Thank you," she whispered.

She rushed out the door, headed to the stables. Her mare was there still saddled. Throwing caution to the wind, she pushed forward, determined to catch up to Walter, her strength gathered from her father's blessing. She had it in her power to make everything right, and she would not waste a moment in doing just that.

CHAPTER 16

WALTER SHOULD HAVE KNOWN Patience's parents would never accept him. Especially after putting Patience in harm's way. Walter silently cursed as he rode home, leading Apollo at a leisurely pace. He didn't want to face his mother and sister after everything that had transpired. He didn't wish to recount the dismal discovery Patience had made.

Daniel murdered to get Walter out of the way. This was his fault. How could he face his family? How could he continue his life without Patience by his side?

This knowledge racked at Walter's consciousness, tearing through his soul. If he had backed out, given up on the case... his brother could be alive now.

No, a voice broke in the back of his head. Daniel would have been killed, regardless. Everyone expecting him to put in a bid for the case. Daniel's murder had been plotted before they had assigned Walter to the Vanderbilt case.

He cursed Lord Danbury and his blatant disregard for human life. Why had no one seen it before? The Baron played his cards right, he'd put on a show for everyone. Walter grit his teeth, tears stinging his eyes as the weight of what he had lost hit him.

Walter stewed in his thoughts. The news would tear his mother and sister apart. He heard the distant pounding of hooves, turning in his saddle as they grew louder, wondering if perhaps Lord Danbury dare show his slimy face. Walter would gladly finish him.

It moved him to see Patience still wearing her blood-stained dress, riding toward him, her face pale in the dimming light of the evening. He stopped, waiting for her to reach his side. She smiled. Her breathless state caused Walter to falter.

"Walter. My papa gave me his blessing."

He stared. Certain he'd misheard. "Your father has agreed to our marriage?"

She laughed and dismounted, and he followed suit, his heart hammering, his spirits lifting with hope. She threw herself into his arms, and he held her tight, feeling her heartbeat against his.

"Papa gave me his blessing after hearing Mama's reasons for refusing you." She pulled away as her voice caught. "She's a selfish woman. I don't know how I can ever forgive her."

Walter couldn't tear his gaze from hers. "Then it's true... we're to be married?"

"Yes, we can be wed," her eyes glistened, a tear escaping. "If you still want me."

His family's finances were in shambles. Even with Patience's dowry, they would need to be creative to pay off the debts. It would be more responsibility, but yes, he still wanted her.

Hang it! He couldn't believe he ever thought of refusing her gift. She'd never given up on him. They'd sell the estate and build a new one if need be. Start a new life in London with his mother and sister. He would reveal Mr. Bamber's role in Daniel's death, and Lord Danbury as the violent, greedy murderer he was. He would continue his career as a barrister.

Perhaps even head barrister.

Walter smiled at his lovely Patience. "I do," he whispered softly. Awed this angel still wanted him.

He dipped his head, planting a soft kiss on her eager lips. Patience arched against him, and he drank her in.

As he pulled away, Patience eyed him. "You must promise never to keep secrets from me again," she chastised him.

He laughed, then sobered as he realized that keeping

secrets from her had almost cost her life. "I promise. I am sorry I did not let you help me sooner."

Patience trailed her hand up his arm, resting it on his shoulder. Her touch lit warmth through his chest. "I forgive you," she whispered.

One last worrying thought troubled Walter's heart. "What about your mother?"

Patience's smile grew forced. "Do not trouble yourself with my mama. She will come to see you as I do—a hard-working, God fearing, respectable gentleman. And if not... she'll miss her grandchildren."

Walter smiled, pulling her closer. "Grandchildren?"

She lifted to her tiptoes, planting another kiss on his lips. "I am yours, Walter Longman. You shall never be rid of me."

He groaned, capturing her lips once more. It was as if they had both been starved of each other as their kisses became more demanding. The barriers between them came down. A spark of wonder ran through him. He didn't deserve her, but he was glad she was here in his arms. He lifted his head. Her cheeks were flushed and her eyes radiant, shining, as if every star had gotten lost in their depths. She was his, forever.

"I love you." Twining his arms around her, he felt for the first time that things would be perfect with Patience by his side.

EPILOGUE

REBECCA ALLEN PRESSED her ear against the parlor door, straining to hear. She rarely eavesdropped, listening behind closed doors. But she had seen Silas Pincock arrive by carriage through her window, watching as he heaved himself out and surveyed her parents' estate. He'd been smacking his lips. A chill ran through her at the memory.

He was revolting, and she knew exactly what he had come for.

They had left the London season in disgrace, when Lord Berkshire discovered her mother's deception. A vile act. She wouldn't believe it involved her mother had she not seen the letter herself. It was her mother's handwriting. She was ashamed. Not that it reflected on her, but that Patience Hawthorn's life had been put in danger, by her mother, for the sake of a titled marriage.

Her mother's voice was smooth and charming, but harder to hear. It was only when Lord Danbury spoke that Rebecca could hear every word.

"Yes, that is a suitable arrangement. Your daughter will suit my needs handsomely." Lord Danbury's thick voice boomed through the door.

Nausea rose in Rebecca's throat.

"Shall we plan for the union next week?" her mother asked pleasantly.

Next week. It had only been a month since their return to the country. All future seasons had vanished. Now her mother was selling her off to the highest bidder. But she didn't know her mother would sacrifice her to the likes of the Baron.

Anger rose in her breast.

"Perhaps sooner, Lady Allen. I'm not getting any younger!" Lord Danbury burst into laughter.

Rebecca's palms grew sweaty. Her head pounded.

"Let us seal the union in two days' time," he continued. "Quiet, no fuss. I understand you and your daughter would like to keep out of the public's eye for the time being."

Rebecca couldn't quite hear her mother's reply. Her voice had dipped into a hushed tone. Her mother should be ashamed. She ruined any chance of a reputable marriage, and destroyed the reputation of other young ladies, a rumor she hadn't believed. She would never forgive her.

"Excellent!" Lord Danbury's voice boomed through the door. "We will be wed in two days, then."

She couldn't stand here any longer. Pushing the door open, she moved into the room, not caring of the impropriety of listening at the door, intruding unannounced. Her reputation was already in shreds.

"Mama, no!" she cried...

THANK YOU FOR READING Patience and Walter's story.

To find out what happens next, read Rebecca's story HERE on Amazon.

Reviews are welcome and appreciated!

ABOUT THE AUTHOR

As Karen Lynne, I write sweet historical romances, regency period being my favorite.

I love history and have been reading hundreds of romances since high school. Timeless authors where the hero and heroine are virtuous with sweet happy endings.

When I am not writing, I enjoy time with my sweetheart, my children and grandchildren and long lunches with my two reading buddies. You know who you are.

Gardening vegetables and fruits in my garden and living in our 1863 stone cottage in the Rocky Mountains.

Life is good!

Printed in Great Britain
by Amazon